She's About That Life: Familiar Territory

By: Keisha Elle

She's About That Life: Familiar Territory – Keisha Elle

She's About That Life: Familiar Territory – Keisha Elle

To my partner, my love, my confidant, my shoulder to lean on, my voice of reason, my

motivator, my biggest supporter…

Thank you for loving me – flaws and all.

She's About That Life: Familiar Territory – Keisha Elle

She's About That Life: Familiar Territory – Keisha Elle

Acknowledgments

All praise must go to the Father above. Thank you for blessing me with the gift of an imagination, and the ability to put my ideas into words.

Thank you Jahquel, for giving me a platform to make my dream a reality.

Thank you to all the authors, editors, and proofreaders who have helped me on my journey. I appreciate you all more than you will ever know!

Thank you Trinette, for motivating me to finish this book. Even when I thought I couldn't do it, you pushed me. This has been a long time coming!

To my tribe of future football players, models, and business owners (yeah, we got big dreams over here), thank you for giving me 'mommy time.' You all realized how important this was for me. I love each and every one of you more than words could ever express.

To the readers, thank you for giving my first novel a

chance. I hope you enjoy!

Keisha

She's About That Life: Familiar Territory – Keisha Elle

Prologue

Asanti placed her hands on her stomach and cried. The slight bulge that she hid under two-size, too big clothing, still protruded outward. Sitting Indian style on the thin, overly used hospital mattress, she lowered her head, allowing the tears to dampen the neck area of her hospital gown.

She grabbed her cell phone off the wheeled tray table. She was glad that she took the phone out of her purse before tossing the almost empty bag in the only chair in the room. Her purse was now out of arms reach, but her cell phone was where it always remained – close by.

Looking at the silenced phone, she wasn't surprised. No missed calls. Only a text message from her boyfriend Justin. Pressing the envelope icon, she read the message.

She's About That Life: Familiar Territory – Keisha Elle

Something came up. b home late. don't wait up.

order [pizza emoji] 4 dinner.

He wasn't even aware that she knew of his deceit.

Erasing the message without replying, she turned on the rear-facing camera. She didn't have a mirror and knew she probably looked as bad as she felt. She was right. Her honey toned skin appeared pasty with large red blotches on her cheeks and forehead. Dark circles were visible under her puffy red eyes. The remnants of tears still lingered on her eye lids. The bouncy, shoulder length dark curls that took her over two hours to produce were now flat and tangled.

Tossing the phone back on the tray table, Asanti leaned back and extended her legs, ignoring the squeaking sound of the old bed. She let out a long sigh. Tears once again began to fall involuntarily. Why was this happening

7

to her? Why did God choose her to incubate and grow a life only to take it away a short time later? It just wasn't fair. Life was not fair.

A college student by day and part-time customer service rep at night, Asanti knew that the timing was not right to bring a child into the world. She was not where she wanted to be in life physically, emotionally, or financially. She struggled to pay the rent on her studio apartment, and even though Justin, her boyfriend of three years, stayed with her most nights, he rarely contributed anything to her household. Still, she was happy. The flickering dot representing a heartbeat on her first ultrasound confirmed that she was going to be someone's mommy.

At fifteen weeks and one day, she gathered the courage to tell her stepbrother her big news. A loner by nature, she didn't have many friends. Out of the family she

She's About That Life: Familiar Territory – Keisha Elle

had left, Shawn was the only one that kept in constant

communication with her. Although they weren't technically

blood related, he was as close to her as a sibling could be.

Being that they lived six hours apart, it was easy for her to

keep her secret. Now that she had surpassed twelve weeks,

the literature that she read told her that she was past the

critical period and less likely to miscarry. She could already

picture the disappointment in his big brown eyes. Shawn

made no secret about his dislike of Justin. He told Asanti

numerous times that she could do better. Now that she was

pregnant, that only ensured that Justin would be a

permanent fixture in her life.

Asanti never got the chance to share her news.

Hours before, she was alone in her apartment, flipping

through channels on the television. Justin's phone chirped,

indicating a text message. The location of the phone deep

in the side of the couch let her know that it was not left

She's About That Life: Familiar Territory – Keisha Elle

intentionally. She retrieved the phone, entered the code that she had memorized, and watched as the phone granted her access.

The text message was from "Wifey". Asanti pressed the envelope icon and read the message.

I miss u baby [sad face emoji]. When r u coming over?

Her calm demeanor quickly turned to rage with every word that she read. Who the hell was 'Wifey'? She hadn't sent him any recent messages.

Asanti tried her best to keep her emotions under control for the sake of her unborn child, but that shit was easier said than done. She went on the attack, using Justin's unoccupied side of the bed as her victim. Hitting the bed like a mad woman, she sobbed uncontrollably. Not only had Justin acted a damn fool when he found out that Asanti

She's About That Life: Familiar Territory – Keisha Elle

was pregnant, he turned the tables and tried to blame her. He told her that she got pregnant on purpose just to trap him – even though he barely had a pot to piss in. For over two months, he slept on her couch as punishment for him sexing her raw, knowing she was not on birth control. He tried to make Asanti feel bad when he was the one creeping with another woman.

When she finally took a breath and stopped the physical assault on the bed, her body froze. She thought that she had peed her pants when a gush of bright red blood escaped from deep within. Intense cramps followed shortly after, leaving her reaching for the nearest object to hold on to, and sending her straight to the Emergency Room. On arrival, a quick ultrasound confirmed that the contents of the sac holding her unborn child was now empty. The flickering heartbeat that instantly put her in to mommy-mode was gone.

She's About That Life: Familiar Territory – Keisha Elle

Knock. Knock.

The nurse entered before she was invited in.

"How are you feeling?" she asked popping her gum and mysteriously pulling out a computer, discreetly folded up into one of the shelves. She began typing loudly. Her spiked red hair bobbed like a rooster. She didn't even look in Asanti's direction.

How the fuck does she think I feel? Asanti thought, ignoring her question. Instead, she focused her eyes on the large dry erase board mounted on the tan wall. It displayed the name of the hospital, University of Louisville Medical Center; the room number, 604; her doctor's name, Dr. Nguyen. Wait, who the hell was Dr. Nguyen? The person that came in and delivered the devastating news was Dr. Perkins. Lastly, her nurse's name was displayed – Tonya. *Yeah, this ghetto bitch looked like a Tonya.*

She's About That Life: Familiar Territory – Keisha Elle

"O-kay." The nurse continued. "On a scale of 1 to 10, how would you rate your pain?"

Again, Asanti was silent. Scanning the room like she'd been doing for the past three hours, her eyes stopped on the only piece of wall décor in the small, private room. It was a picture of a vase with a single flower in it. The crack in the middle of the glass was obvious to anyone who took the time to take a look.

"Umm…" The nurse glanced at the computer screen before she began. "A-son-tee." She mispronounced the name. "Look, I can't help you unless you start talking. I'm not a mind reader." She chewed her gum loudly, with her mouth open.

Asanti shook her head. She inwardly hoped that a patient questionnaire would be sent to her home. She definitely wanted U of L Hospital to know that they should

She's About That Life: Familiar Territory – Keisha Elle

raise their standards during the hiring process. She would never visit this hospital again.

Asanti lowered her hazel eyes to the tiled floor below, as a painful cramp grabbed hold of her uterus and squeezed it for dear life. When the pain finally subsided, she exhaled loudly and focused her eyes back on the ugly pattern. It reminded her of the cheap linoleum flooring that used to line her grandmother's bathroom. It probably had been on sale.

"Everything looks okay." The nurse said, clicking the computer mouse repeatedly. "Oh, your discharge has already been processed. You can leave whenever you're ready." She returned the computer back to its previous position. "But we do have patient's waiting in the ER. The sooner you get ready, the faster someone else can get this room." She turned around and began walking toward the

She's About That Life: Familiar Territory – Keisha Elle

closed wood door. "If you need anything, let me know."

Opening the door, she halted when she heard Asanti's

voice.

"Tonya, wait." She loudly cleared her throat. "So

what am I supposed to do now?" Asanti's voice cracked as

she spoke.

The nurse halted in the doorway and turned on her

heels. Her bright pink Nike shoes made a loud squeaking

sound.

"I'm Natia. Tonya is on first shift."

Asanti was too through! She regretted the question

as soon as Natia opened her mouth again.

"Look, you're a young girl. You've been given an

opportunity to do you without having someone else to

depend on. This may be a blessing in disguise." She walked

over and stood at Asanti's bedside. "You really want to

know what you should do now?" She raised an eyebrow, anticipating Asanti's answer.

"Yes."

Natia bent down so close to Asanti that the smell of her cinnamon flavored gum overwhelmed her senses.

"It's simple. You live."

She's About That Life: Familiar Territory – Keisha Elle

Chapter 1

Asanti stared at the letter again in disbelief. Three years. Three fucking years and the undeniable truth was gazing back at her. How could she be so stupid? She thought about all the times that he told her he loved her. He said she was the only one for him. He was going to give her his last name and make it official one day. The other women were just friends. They didn't mean anything. He was just a likeable guy. Bullshit! Even a story concocted by the late Johnny Cochran couldn't change the verdict in this situation. No matter how you twisted the words or changed things around, DNA didn't lie. Justin was the father. Her best friend, her provider, her man, had expanded his family with another woman. The proof of Justin's betrayal was like a dagger to Asanti's heart. It was too much for her young soul to bare.

She's About That Life: Familiar Territory – Keisha Elle

Adjusting herself in her window seat of the noisy Greyhound, she folded the letter neatly and placed it back in her oversized black tote. A whirlwind of emotions ran through her as a loud sigh escaped her lips. She was tired. Not in the physical sense, just tired. Tired of giving more than what she was receiving. Tired of being so close to happiness, yet so far away. Her puffy, red-rimmed eyes were full of pain and sadness, but she refused to let another tear fall.

The various side conversations ceased as the bus pulled in to the Nashville bus station. She was aware of the two-hour layover, and transfer of buses, but reserved her spot anyway. It was the first available bus to leave Louisville that night and Asanti wanted to get the hell away as fast as she could.

A sense of relief fell upon her as she exited the crowded bus. She wasn't sure if it was due to leaving the

She's About That Life: Familiar Territory – Keisha Elle

place she called home for most of her twenty-one years on Earth, or if it was freedom from the overwhelming smell of bad hygiene. Maybe it was the loud voices that couldn't be covered up with the Trey Songz station on Pandora.

She listened to three bad ass heathens yell and scream for over two hours. Their out of control asses were in need of a good ass whooping. She would have gladly lent her bedazzled belt to discipline the bad ass kids, but the woman sitting beside them with fire engine red hair and a bull nose ring, was equally loud and obnoxious. She noticed that on one of her countless phone conversations. It was a lost cause.

"I hope they're not on the next bus," Asanti said to herself, waiting for her single red suitcase to be pulled from the luggage compartment. She looked around in embarrassment realizing that she spoke her thoughts out loud.

She's About That Life: Familiar Territory – Keisha Elle

"I was thinking the same thing," a voice responded, walking past Asanti to retrieve a black leather Tumi packing case and duffle bag that matched the one she carried over her shoulder. Turning to Asanti, she added, "If I have to listen to that noise from here to Atlanta, I'm going to scream." The girls exchanged a friendly laugh.

Noticing her bag, Asanti walked over, inspected it, and released the handle, allowing it roll behind her on its small wheels. She walked back over to the friendly girl still occupying the same space.

"My name's Asanti by the way. I'm going to Atlanta too." She usually wouldn't engage in a conversation with a stranger, but right now Asanti was just happy to see a welcoming face.

"I'm Komiko," the girl said with a smile.

Asanti noticed a set of perfect white teeth. Every black hair on Komiko's head was securely fastened in her

She's About That Life: Familiar Territory – Keisha Elle

high bun. Her tall, lean frame was enviable, and the texture of her almond colored skin looked as soft as a baby's bottom. Standing before her in a beaded romper and high wedged heels, Komiko belonged on a runway, instead of a Greyhound.

Asanti immediately looked down at her ill-fitting t-shirt and jeans. Her amazing curves were hidden under the excess material.

"You look like you've had a long day," Komiko said looking from the bottom of Asanti's cheap thong flip flops to her loose, messy ponytail.

"You have no idea." Asanti attempted to push a stray piece of hair back into its rightful place. It was no use. In an attempt to leave in a hurry, she neglected to shower, change clothes, or even comb her hair. Accepting defeat, she removed the black hair tie and let her natural brown ringlets fall.

She's About That Life: Familiar Territory – Keisha Elle

"We have time," Komiko said, looking down at the gold Movado watch wrapped around her tiny wrist. "It's still a long way to Atlanta."

Asanti let out a long sigh. *Maybe it would be nice to talk to someone*, she thought. The chances of ever seeing Komiko again were slim to none, so there was nothing to lose. Spotting a place to sit back and relax, Asanti nodded toward an empty wooden bench. Komiko looked in the direction of Asanti's nod. The bench was old, and the metal on the arms and legs were slightly rusted. It would have to do. Poor lighting distracted others from migrating to the area. Quickly surveying the surroundings one last time, Asanti and Komiko grabbed their belongings and strolled down the concrete path toward the bench.

Sitting down and crossing one leg over the other, Asanti observed the night sky. The flickering stars were calming and tranquil. She envisioned connecting the dots,

She's About That Life: Familiar Territory – Keisha Elle

creating an array of different images. The cool, late spring air combined with a slight breeze, made it a beautiful night.

"Have you ever just wanted to give up?" Asanti asked, lowing her eyes from the dark sky above and looking Komiko square in the eyes. Without waiting for a response, she continued. "That's exactly how I feel right now. I don't even know where I'm going. I just needed to get away." With slight hesitation, she opened up and let her words tell her pained story.

*****

Growing up in the streets of Louisville, KY, Asanti had it hard. Her Hispanic mother, Julissa Hernandez, grew up in Louisville after migrating there with her parents as a young child. She quickly became accustomed to the fast life in her early teenage years after several stints of running away. Unable to be controlled by her overly strict parents, she quit school and left home in an effort to assert her independence. When she found herself pregnant at the tender age of sixteen, she returned home, trying to put her life back together. It was short lived. Her stitches weren't even healed before she was back at it again, leaving her aging parents to raise her newborn daughter.

Asanti thrived with her grandparents. She enjoyed the luxury of a two parent household in a decent section of town. She was always on the honor roll at school and shined on the local debate team at school. Regardless of the topic, she could always argue her way to a victory.

Her father, David McCoy, was a successful lawyer in Atlanta. He met Julissa when she lived in Louisville. His father was one of the few Black entrepreneurs in the area, owning a corner store in the section of town that Julissa lived. He frequently helped his father in the store after school. He noticed Julissa the first time she came in. The

She's About That Life: Familiar Territory – Keisha Elle

words rolling off her tongue in her slight, Spanish accent turned him on. He began stealing glances at her every time she came in. When she accidentally brushed up against him one day and his dick stood straight up in his pants, he knew he had to have her. That night he did just that, busting his first nut, not at his own expense. He fucked her almost every day after that, until one day his family unexpectedly relocated to Atlanta with very little notice. Julissa lost touch with David before she could tell him that he was going to be a dad. He went to college and eventually law school before finding out about Asanti.

Julissa returned home once again after a car accident claimed the lives of her parents. For the first time in eleven years, she attempted to step up and be a mother to Asanti. She received a hefty insurance check for her parent's death. It was gone before the ink dried on her signature. The drug habit that she'd acquired took control

She's About That Life: Familiar Territory – Keisha Elle

of both her body, and her finances. Without a job and a legitimate way of earning money, she moved into two-bedroom apartment in the Park Hill projects. She was adapting well to motherhood for a while, but it didn't fit well with her fast lifestyle. Choosing a man over her daughter, she left her child to fend for herself and relocated to Lexington chasing someone else's husband. Child protective services stepped in and removed Asanti, after it was reported that she had been left alone for several days. She was placed into the foster care system.

Asanti was placed with a well-to-do family outside of the city. The couple had a son, Justin, who took an immediate liking to the pretty young thing. Even though he was three years older, he liked spending time with Asanti. The physical attraction that he had toward her upon meeting was growing into an emotional one as well. Four years after meeting her, he busted her fifteen-year-old

She's About That Life: Familiar Territory – Keisha Elle

cherry late one night when his parents were sleeping comfortably in their beds.

Justin took his time, stopping occasionally to ensure that her first time wasn't entirely painful. The sting of her innocence being torn away was replaced by pure bliss when he withdrew from her aching hole and explored her pussy with his tongue. Ignoring the metallic taste of blood, he let his tongue travel freely. He licked the opening to her hole and flickered his tongue on her clit. When he inserted two fingers and sucked hard on her rosebud, he tasted her orgasm. Replacing his fingers with his throbbing dick, he entered her again. He was slow and gentle. Her soft moans were music to his ears as he rhythmically timed each firm stroke. Her tight pussy wrapped around his dick like a glove. He tried to hold out, but it was a lost cause. Feeling his seed rise, he withdrew quickly and released the milky white substance on her stomach.

She's About That Life: Familiar Territory – Keisha Elle

From that day on, the two hooked up every chance they could. Asanti was getting sexed on the regular until one day, a social worker came and sent Asanti packing on a plane. After sixteen years, David was introduced to his daughter. A chance encounter brought him back to his hometown, where he ran into Julissa and learned about Asanti. Julissa looked bad, heavily strung out on drugs. It didn't seem to faze her that her daughter was with another family. When David returned to Atlanta, he filed the necessary paperwork to have Asanti removed from foster care and place with him.

Asanti stayed with her father until she graduated. Often clashing with his new wife, and stepsister, it had become too much to handle. She would miss her father and stepbrother, Shawn, but felt that it would be best. After graduating, she ran right back to Louisville, and back into Justin's bed. She had kept in contact with him over the

She's About That Life: Familiar Territory – Keisha Elle

years, promising to come back when she finished school. She kept her promise.

Justin and Asanti moved in together, and made their relationship official. They moved around several times before eventually renting an apartment in the West End of the city. The surroundings weren't the best, but they were manageable. The neighborhood was situated in a predominately Black area. The location was more ideal for Justin. To keep money in his pockets, he began selling weed. Most of his clientele was in a ten block radius, and that suited Justin just fine.

Asanti was living life, hoping to make a name for herself and eventually move to a better part of the city. In three years, she graduated from the University of Louisville with a Bachelor's Degree in Economics. Her progression toward Graduate School halted when she found herself

She's About That Life: Familiar Territory – Keisha Elle

pregnant. Determined not to become a statistic, Asanti enrolled in Graduate School anyway. Even after the loss of her child, she remained optimistic.

That all changed when Asanti retrieved the mail that fateful day. A manila envelope addressed to Justin Black from the Division of Child Enforcement caught her eye. Sitting the thick stack of letters and advertisements aside, she opened Justin's mail. There it was in black and white. Justin was the father of five-month old Cori Jones. To add insult to injury, the next page of the stapled document included a picture of the chubby cheeked baby, with eyes matching her man's.

Wiping away her fallen tears, Asanti retrieved a large red suitcase from the walk-in closet. She stuffed the suitcase with as many clothes and personal hygiene products that would fit. Once it was filled to capacity, she grabbed the bag, her purse and cell phone and did something she hadn't done in years – rode public transportation. When the city bus stopped in front of the Greyhound station, Asanti hopped off and bought a ticket for the next bus leaving. She had an hour before the bus heading to Atlanta, GA by way of Nashville, TN was scheduled to depart.

Using the downtime to think about her life, Asanti was determined to make a change. A fresh start was just what she needed to find herself. She wanted true happiness and hoped that Atlanta would give her that. Life had to be better than this.

Chapter 2

"Well, here it is," Komiko said opening the door to her seventh floor condo. "Mi casa es su casa."

She's About That Life: Familiar Territory – Keisha Elle

"Gracias," Asanti said with a smile, stepping in and immediately admiring the spacious layout. A dark purple accent wall stood out amongst the other off white walls. It was lined with a neat row of black and white still headshots of Komiko. Each photo displayed a different expression.

A large black shag run covered the dark wood floor. Two lime green swivel accent chairs and a tan couch set atop a black rug. With lots of pillows adorning them in various designs of black and white, the arrangement was odd to Asanti. She was used to matching couches and loveseats with plain walls. Komiko's place displayed her unique style. Everything was strategically placed in the middle of the room. The outer perimeter was still readily available to move around.

She's About That Life: Familiar Territory – Keisha Elle

"Take a look around," Komiko said gesturing for Asanti to freely roam the condo. Taking her advice, she did.

After pouring her heart out to Komiko at the Greyhound station, Asanti sat with a puzzled look on her face. Reality sat in when she realized that she had nowhere to go. Her father didn't know that she was back in town. She didn't want to just show up at his doorstep after only calling for Holidays and Birthdays. She thought about calling Shawn. They had established a strong brother/sister bond. Out of everyone in her life, he was the only one who never let her down. She sent him a quick text instead.

Hey, I'm in town call me when you can. I [heart emoji] U.

Not knowing why she did it, Komiko invited Asanti to crash at her place. Maybe it was the desperate look on her face. Or maybe it was the fact that just not long ago, she was in the same predicament.

"This is a nice place you have here," Asanti said turning the corner back into the living room. "It must cost a fortune to live in something like this."

"I manage," Komiko said modestly. Although she was financially secure, she was never one to advertise it. She would have enjoyed a nice comfortable seat in first class traveling back to Atlanta, but she opted for the quickest ride at that time – Greyhound. The next flight wasn't leaving until early the next morning. She wanted to be in her comfy bed before the sun came up.

"Well, I hope to be like you when I grow up," Asanti said sarcastically.

"I believe everything happens for reason," Komiko said walking into her large open kitchen. Asanti followed

She's About That Life: Familiar Territory – Keisha Elle

behind quietly, taking a seat around the circular glass table. "Maybe I can help you follow your dreams, so you can be like me when you grow up." Komiko smiled widely. In the hours the two spent together on the bus ride to Atlanta, they really learned a lot about each other.

Komiko walked over and retrieved two bottled waters from her refrigerator and sat down in a chair across from Asanti. Opening it, she took a long swig and sat the bottle back down.

"Tomorrow, I'll get in contact with my brother. If I'm going to be living here, I have to find a job," Asanti said, breaking the silence and taking a sip of her water.

"Where are you going?" Komiko asked curiously.

"I don't know. I guess I'll just look around and see what's out there." Asanti took another sip of her water.

She's About That Life: Familiar Territory – Keisha Elle

"I know somebody," Komiko began, looking into Asanti's eyes. "His name is Rico and he owes me a favor." A confused look appeared on Asanti's face, so Komiko explained further. "He owns a club on the other side of town. He's always looking for new talent, and you have a beautiful face…"

"A stripper," Asanti said cutting Komiko off. "You want me to be a stripper?"

"I want you to be independent." Komiko did not mean anything negative by her suggestion. "I have no problem with you staying here until you get straight with your family. I think it will be mad cool having someone around. But I know you want more. Just think about it. Sometimes you have to do what you don't want to do in order to do what you want to do. Remember that."

She's About That Life: Familiar Territory – Keisha Elle

Asanti thought about Komiko's words carefully.
Stripper? Really? Although Asanti was comfortable in her
own skin, stripping never crossed her mind. She gave
Komiko a shy smile. She wasn't even going to entertain the
idea of taking her clothes off for money. Dancing was easy,
but was a whole new ball game. There was a big difference.
Dancing required skilled, time, and dedication. It was an
art. Stripping was selling sex. Nothing more. Nothing less.

"I don't know," Asanti said softly.

"It's just a thought," Komiko said, standing up with
authority. She could see the apprehension in Asanti's face.
"Come on, let's take a ride. I want to show you a couple of
things."

Asanti was happy to get off the subject.
Straightening up the rags covering her body, she followed
behind Komiko as she led the way to her brand new

She's About That Life: Familiar Territory – Keisha Elle

Mercedes CLS 550 Coupe. Her body slid down against the comfortable leather seats. It still had the unforgettable "new car" smell.

Asanti enjoyed the scenery as Komiko pulled up in front of a strip mall. Parking in a space directly in front of a door with a brightly lit sign with the words NAIL SALON, the pair walked in. Bypassing the makeshift waiting area of six chairs against the glass window, Asanti followed Komiko to a row of massage chairs with pedicure bowls attached. Sitting in the first chair, Komiko turned the jets on, placed her feet in the once idle water, and sat down. Asanti rolled up her pant legs and followed without hesitation.

"Hello, Ms. Williams," a woman said with a strong Vietnamese accent. Coming from a room in the back of the building, she opened a clear jar, and scooped a blue bath

She's About That Life: Familiar Territory – Keisha Elle

salt mixture into both pedicure bowls with a small black spoon. "You late."

"I got back in town later than expected." Turning to Asanti and back to the woman, she added, "This is Asanti. Asanti this is Vy."

"Hi," Asanti said fiddling with the chair's remote control. Finding an acceptable setting, she repositioned herself and enjoyed the firm massage on her back.

"You let feet soak," Vy said in broken English. Walking away to retrieve her pedicure tools, she instantly disappeared into the back.

"That feels good," Asanti mouthed out loud, enjoying the underwater foot massage her feet were experiencing. A short Vietnamese woman sat down at the foot of the pedicure bowl and nodded. With gloved hands,

She's About That Life: Familiar Territory – Keisha Elle

she reached under the water and began massaging Asanti's heel.

Sitting in the black massage chair with the rollers going up and down her spine, Asanti was in heaven. All of the day's tension spontaneously left her body. She was enjoying the pampering at her newfound friend's expense.

"I get this twice a week," Komiko said knocking Asanti out of her almost orgasmic trance. "Every Wednesday and Saturday.

Asanti sat up slightly and looked at Komiko. Her head sat back on the headrest with her eyes closed. She looked completely comfortable and at peace. Smiling to herself, she wondered if she would be able to enjoy this lifestyle as well.

Fresh incents masked the smell of acrylic and jasmine. Soft instrumental music could be heard over a

She's About That Life: Familiar Territory – Keisha Elle

faint conversation. Two employees talked amongst themselves in their native language. On the comfortable spring afternoon, Asanti and Komiko were the only patrons.

A large sixty inch LED television graced one of the walls fixed to the local news. The sound was muted but the closed captioning eased any confusion. Breaking news of a house fire caught her attention. She wasn't familiar with the area, but the sad look on the owner's face standing next to her three children touched Asanti's heart.

A bell chimed acknowledging the presence of another patron. A dark skinned woman with an overly curvaceous body strolled in. Her six-inch red bottom heels echoed loudly with each step. The black wrap dress that she wore was emphasized by each sway of her hips. She was bad! She commanded attention. Not even stopping to wait

She's About That Life: Familiar Territory – Keisha Elle

for an invitation to the back room, she disappeared behind a door almost as quickly as she entered.

"That's Naomi," Komiko said hearing the lock turn on the door the girl walked through. "She's goes by Envy at Club Fantasy."

"Club Fantasy?" Asanti questioned.

"Yeah. That's the spot I was telling you about. She dances there. I don't know her personally, but according to Rico, she's his cash cow."

Asanti let out a jealous smirk. The girl was definitely cute, but Asanti had her beat by a mile in the looks department. She thought about it and shook her head. There wasn't an amount of money large enough that could make her take her clothes off.

She's About That Life: Familiar Territory – Keisha Elle

She's About That Life: Familiar Territory – Keisha Elle

Chapter 3

Shawn pulled his Black Mercedes S class into the driveway of his parent's gated home. Asanti looked on in amazement as the large steel gates parted to let his luxury car in. It was a big upgrade from the home she previously lived in with her father. Since Asanti left Atlanta, David started his own firm, partnering with one of his law school buddies. Within a couple of years, Rainwater & McCoy, LLC was the top entertainment law firm in the South, bringing in a lot of money for the two owners. After Shawn graduated law school earlier in the year, he joined his stepfather David, along with Jackson Rainwater's son Jace, and turned the business into a family affair. Once the money started rolling in, he upgraded from a 3,000 square foot home to the over 7,000 square foot mini-mansion Asanti was now staring up at. David McCoy took 'balling' to a different level.

She's About That Life: Familiar Territory – Keisha Elle

Shawn had called Asanti back less than two hours after she texted him. He was more than ecstatic that she was back in town. He agreed to meet up with her the next day, which was why they were now sitting in her father's driveway. They spent time catching up at Komiko's place. After reminiscing on the goods times, Shawn convinced her to go see her father. Too much time had passed since they last laid eyes on each other.

Shawn parked his car in the large driveway and started walking towards the large wood and glass entry door. Asanti followed, her nerves relaxing at the darkened house. Every light was turned off except for the bright light beaming off the large porch. It was apparent that everyone was sleep or not home.

"I don't think anyone's home. We can come back later."

She's About That Life: Familiar Territory – Keisha Elle

"They're home. They usually park in the garage."

The mention of 'they' reminded Asanti of her stepmother. She was the reason for the strained relationship with her father. When David showed any type of attention toward Asanti, Cynthia would become jealous. Although David was not the biological father of her children, she felt that Asanti was intruding on their good thing. David was too blind to see the chaos and confusion that his wife was causing. When his daughter couldn't take it anymore and left shortly after graduation, he attributed it to her assertion of independent. When the phone calls slowed down and ceased all together, he assumed that his daughter just needed her space. He backed off, but kept the line of communication open. If she ever needed him, she could always call.

She's About That Life: Familiar Territory — Keisha Elle

Shawn fidgeted with his keys until he found the correct one. He slowly inserted it and walked inside. Asanti stopped in the doorway. It was pitch black. She didn't know her way around the dark, unfamiliar setting.

"Turn on the light." Asanti felt the wall with her left hand in an effort to find the light switch. The bright light flicked on before she could locate it.

"Surprise!"

Breathtaking fear momentarily overwhelmed her, causing her nerves to become unraveled. The initial shock of the yelling voices scared her so bad that she dropped the small clutch purse that she held in her hand. Struggling to gain her composure, she gave a shy smile before a crowd of people engulfed her.

"Welcome back Baby Girl," David said smiling. He was the first one to reach her. He wrapped his big arms around her before she could even respond. The embrace was tight and welcoming. An unspoken apology passed through them. It had been way too many years of not speaking.

"You don't know how good it is to see you dad." Asanti couldn't hold back the tears welling up in her eyes. "I really missed you."

"I missed you too Baby Girl. You're home now, that's all that matters."

"Ok, that's enough," a female voice interjected. "She's my sister too!"

Asanti turned her gaze towards the slim, girl with smooth milk chocolate skin. She was a spitting image of her mother, which wasn't necessarily a good thing. The cocky attitude to match was definitely a turn off. The two always bumped heads, reluctant to accept the fact that marriage made them sisters. Unfortunately, you can't choose your family.

"Hi Sidney," Asanti said nonchalantly.

"Oh, I can't get a hug?" The sarcasm was evident in Sidney's voice.

"Sure." Asanti put on a fake smile and opened her arms, anticipating the quick, loose hug. She didn't want to show out in front of the room full of people. When Asanti felt the firm grip of her stepsister's arms wrapping around her shoulders, she was genuinely surprised.

Sidney leaned her head against Asanti's and whispered in her ear.

"I don't know why you're here, but I intend on finding out." She released her embrace and took a step back. The same fake smile was still planted on her face. Without another word, she turned on her heels and walked off. Asanti didn't know what to make of the situation, but a mental note was etched in her mind. She was definitely going to watch that sneaky bitch.

Several more hugs and kind words followed before Asanti had a moment to herself. She was bombarded with old friends from the neighborhood and distant family members all up in her grill. Even her stepmother came by and offered a fake hug. She was glad when the newness of her arrival wore off and everyone began mingling amongst each other.

The large two-story home was exquisite. The huge Great Room contained nineteen foot ceilings and oversized furniture. It was decorated in her stepmother's bland style, although the hardwood floors were shined to perfection. A large projection screen displayed a collection of music videos and doubled as the entertainment for the night. The

She's About That Life: Familiar Territory – Keisha Elle

absence of alcohol prevented everyone from getting turnt up, but everyone appeared to be having a good time.

Asanti's long hair flowed as she walked around, catching up on old times with one of her numerous cousins. Her short, white mid-thigh romper hugged every curve of her body for dear life. The rest of her attire was simple, calf-length gladiator sandals, hoop earrings, and an assortment of bangles on her left wrist. She was laughing loudly at something her cousin said when she felt a tap on her shoulder. Turning around, her face flushed and her voice became trapped in her throat.

Jace Rainwater stood with a small bouquet of red roses. His Kodak smile was perfect as usual. His deep cocoa complexion was flawless. He had more facial hair than she remembered. His struggling mustache was now replaced with a full, well-groomed mustache and goatee.

She's About That Life: Familiar Territory – Keisha Elle

He wore strong smelling cologne. It entered her nostrils and pierced her heart. His dark eyes were hard to read, but the smile on his face let her know that he was happy to be there.

"What do you want?" Asanti asked coldly.

"Welcome back." He smiled softly before extending the red roses in her direction. "I got these for you."

"I don't want them," Asanti said with a straight face, never taking her eyes off him.

"Ummm…," her cousin began, looking like a deer staring into a pair of bright headlights. "I'll be back." She could tell that shit was about to get real and she wanted no part of it. She hurried off in the direction of the catered food.

"Take the flowers Asanti. They're a gift." The hurt was evident in his dark eyes.

She's About That Life: Familiar Territory – Keisha Elle

"I don't want anything from you! Why are you even here?"

Asanti's relevated voice caught the attention of her father. He caught up to the pair in five long strides. He greeted Jace warmly and turned to his daughter.

"Is everything ok?"

"No, it's not. Daddy why is he here?" A warm batch of tears filled her eyes and threatened to fall. She refused to let him see her cry.

"I invited him." David stuck his hands in the pockets of his dark jeans. He was unaware of the tension between his daughter and Jace. "I invited everyone that you used to hang out with. Is there a problem with that?"

Asanti turned head in her father's direction but her eyes remained on Jace. She gave him a hard side-eye before rolling her eyes with much attitude. She couldn't believe that he had the audacity to show up after he caused her so much pain years ago.

"Asanti, I'm sorry about the way things ended when you left." Sincerity could be heard in his voice. He lowered his tone, just above a whisper. "I've apologized time and time again. I tried calling when you left, but you never returned any of my calls."

"Maybe you should take a hint. Go to hell Jace! And take your damn roses with you!" She threw the roses down at his feet and stormed off in the opposite direction.

"Asanti!" Her father called after her.

She didn't even stop to acknowledge him, as she stomped up the stairs. She didn't know the layout of the house, or even where she was going, but she had to get away. Her surprise party was a big fucking disaster.

*****

She's About That Life: Familiar Territory – Keisha Elle

Asanti sat alone on the steps leading up to her father's house. After calling Komiko, she patiently waited for her friend to arrive. She wish she could have rescinded Shawn's invitation and stayed home instead. A million thoughts ran through her head as she relived the day's events. She knew that her path would cross with Jace, but she didn't expect it to happen so soon. In truth, her heart never recovered from the emotional diss that he tossed her way. He used her. When he got what he wanted he threw her out like a pile of trash.

She was young and that shit was the worst pain that she had ever experienced. It was worse than breaking an arm or a leg. Feelings and emotions are something a cast can't hold into place.

They were feeling each other – hard. It didn't take long for seventeen-year-old Asanti to fall for twenty-year-

She's About That Life: Familiar Territory – Keisha Elle

old Jace. He was her brother's best friend and an honorary member of the McCoy household. He spent so much time over there that no one would have noticed if he moved all of his belongings in.

Jace was immediately drawn to Asanti. She was beautiful in his eyes and she actually had brain too, unlike many of the girls he know. She would join in his conversations and offer a different perspective on things. She stimulated his mind, followed by his heart shortly after. Jace wanted to explore deeper, but that had the potential of blowing up in his face. David trust him, and treated him almost like a son. Jace didn't want to disrespect him like that.

It was easy for Jace to ignore her at first. He told himself that Asanti was a little girl, and that made her off limits. He waved off her innocent flirting and played it

She's About That Life: Familiar Territory – Keisha Elle

cool, but the more time he spent around her, the more intrigued he became. She had goals and dreams. He would sit up and talk to her damn near the whole night outside on her father's porch. He learned that after high school, Asanti wanted to go to college and make something of herself. He was a junior in college, and shared some of his college experiences with her.

Late one summer night, Jace heard a knock at his door. He was sitting on his couch, enjoying his first night in his new apartment. When he opened the door and saw Asanti, he immediately let her in.

"What's wrong?" he asked, seeing the desperate look on her face.

"I just needed to get away."

Asanti walked in and took over the seat Jace once occupied.

She's About That Life: Familiar Territory – Keisha Elle

"I got into it with Sidney."

Jace didn't need to hear any more. He knew about all about their strained relationship. They took the term sister rivalry to a whole new level. If one had something, the other wanted it. They would do things just to make the other one mad. No one truly knew why they had animosity towards each other. Everyone thought they would grow out of it as they matured; however, it was getting much worse, and fast.

He walked over and took a seat next to Asanti. He really hated seeing her like that. Her pretty face had red blotches, and he could tell she had been crying.

"You can chill her for a while. I'll take you home when you're ready."

Asanti inched closer to him on the couch, allowing her leg to touch his. She placed her soft hand on his knee

58

She's About That Life: Familiar Territory – Keisha Elle

and gazed deep into his eyes. Her heart was racing and by the uncomfortable look that spread across his face, she knew his was racing too.

"Can I stay?" she asked.

Jace contemplated her question. He wanted to say no, but the words couldn't escape his lips. When he didn't respond, Asanti asked again. She moved her hand upward and stopped when she felt the head of his dick resting comfortably on his thigh. A low exhalation breath escaped her lips.

The feel of her hand excited him in a way that he couldn't explain. She was only sixteen, but she definitely knew what she wanted. He struggled with his conscience, but his growing erection made the ultimate decision. Noticing the slow rise in his pants, she removed her sandals and lifted her tight shirt over her head. It was on.

She's About That Life: Familiar Territory – Keisha Elle

Leaning in, he allowed his lips to meet hers. He parted her lips with his tongue and entered slowly. She didn't resist. Leaving her mouth, she trailed small kisses down the side of her face and neck. When he reached her black lace bra, he softly kissed her protruding nipples. Asanti moaned. Reaching back, he unfastened her bra and freed her breasts. They were perky and firm. Her tan areolas had small, hardened pebbles in the center. He took one into his mouth. He hungrily licked and sucked her nipple, stopping only to show the same love to the other one. Asanti panted and moaned in ecstasy. He left her breasts and made a trail of kissed down her tight stomach. He kissed and swirled his tongue inside her navel.

"Are you sure you want this?"

"Yes," she said, nodding at the same time.

She's About That Life: Familiar Territory – Keisha Elle

"Stand up," he commanded, lifting his shirt over his head.

When she stood, he dropped to his knees and pulled down her shorts and panties in one swift motion. He sat back on his knees admiring the beautiful body that stood before him. *Damn*, he said under his breath.

Jace pushed her back into a sitting position on the couch. He eased her legs open, exposing a glistening, hairless pussy. She was already wet. Licking his lips, he lowered his head and devoured her sweet middle.

Asanti arched her back and moaned loudly. Never in her wildest dreams did she think that her body could feel so good. She grabbed the back of the couch, needing something firm to hold on to. He was eating her so good that it wasn't long before her legs began to tremble and her warm juices gushed out. Jace licked every drop.

She's About That Life: Familiar Territory – Keisha Elle

He sat up, his face still wet with her juices. Asanti swallowed hard, still panting from her explosive orgasm. His tongue game was on point. When Jace stood up and walked away, confusion was etched on her face. She was ready to deepthroat his pole and show him the same attention he gave her. Jace had other plans. He returned a short time later with his dick wrapped up, and ready to go. He eased her legs onto the couch and climbed on top of her.

"Just relax," he whispered, nearing the head of his penis toward her opening. Without saying another word, he thrust into her, stretching her open to accommodate his massive girth.

Asanti closed her eyes, enjoying the moment. Jace was an unselfish lover, and took his time with each slow stroke.

She's About That Life: Familiar Territory – Keisha Elle

"Look at me," Jace said, planting small kisses on her lips.

Asanti obliged, opening her eyes to see Jace peering down at her. The moment was intense and special at the same time. Not only was Jace giving it to her better than she ever had, the emotions alone far exceeded her wildest dreams. Jace didn't need to say anything. She felt it. Each slow thrust from his thick, black dick, was pure bliss. The feel of their sweaty bodies pounding against each other caused another orgasm to brew inside her. She exploded, digging her nails into his back and loudly yelling his name. He released his nut deep inside her before collapsing on top of her.

They began having sex on a regular basis. They were smart enough to keep things discreet. No one suspected that the two were getting it in. Asanti loved the way Jace made her body feel. She knew that when she left his apartment, her pussy would be throbbing and a big ass grin would be plastered across her face.

But all good things come to an end. She was comfortably sprawled across her bed when Sidney softly knocked on the door. Sidney slowly walked in, with a mischevious smile forming on her face.

"What do you want?"

The sisters had quickly grown distant towards each other, but Asanti was not really sure why. When they first met, Sidney was happy to have another female in the house around her age. They dropped the 'step' from their titles and introduce themselves as sisters. When David began showing Asanti more attention, Sidney got jealous. It wasn't that he was showing favoritism. He had been a part of Sidney's life since she was two-years-old. He didn't get

She's About That Life: Familiar Territory – Keisha Elle

Asanti until she was sixteen. He was trying to make up for

lost time. Sidney didn't see it that way. She began

sabotaging everything that Asanti did. When Asanti did

chores, Sidney would go behind her and mess things up.

Shortly after, she would tell her mother, just so Asanti

would get punished. She repeatedly lied on Asanti, telling

her parents that she was doing things that weren't true.

When Asanti finally had enough, and went off on her

stepmother for the false accusations, her father stood by his

wife, reprimanding Asanti for being disrespectful. Things

continued to get worse. Asanti was labeled as being a

trouble maker, while Sidney was praised for being a model

child. Now, her number one enemy was standing in her

room with a stupid grin on her face.

"I just wanted to show you something?"

"What?"

She's About That Life: Familiar Territory – Keisha Elle

She whipped her phone out of her pocket in record speed. Typing in a numerical code and pressing the gallery icon, she opened the picture of Shawn standing behind his girlfriend Kat, Sidney with her new boo Caleb, and Jace with his arm around another girl.

"What is this?" Asanti was trying not to let her anger show, but it was a lost cause.

"We all went out last night. You know, like a couples thing. Jace didn't tell you?"

"Why would he tell me anything?"

"I see the way you look at him. If I didn't know any better, I'd say you two were getting it in."

"I don't know what you're talking about."

Sidney laughed, figuring that Asanti wasn't going to confirm her suspicions anyway. Everyone else may have

She's About That Life: Familiar Territory – Keisha Elle

been oblivious to what was going on, but not Sidney. She peeped that shit from day one. Jace and Asanti were spending way too much time together to just be friends. Sidney was jealous. Jace was occupying Asanti's time, leaving Sidney out in the cold. As retaliation, she began sabotaging everything Asanti did. When her mother, Cynthia, noticed Asanti's slip-ups, it was icing on the cake for Sidney. She had inadvertently caused a rift between the two, that only intensified with time. David tried to be the calming force, but even he began to show signs of frustration towards his daughter.

"We had a great time. Maybe you can come next time. That is, when you get a man."

"Get out of my room."

A devilish grin spread across Sidney's face. She had fulfilled her purpose. Asanti was fuming.

She's About That Life: Familiar Territory – Keisha Elle

"You are so mean. I just came in here to talk to you." She made it a point to speak loudly. She wanted her mother, or even better David, to hear the conversation.

"Get out! Now!"

"Okay. Okay. Geesh, so much for being nice." She taunted Asanti in the doorway. "Have a good night sis."

Jace's number was dialed and his sexy voice was on the other end of the phone before Sidney could close the door. Asanti couldn't hide the hurt in her voice. She was crying before the first word left her mouth.

"You son of a bitch."

"Whoa. Wait. What's going on?"

"I saw the picture you took last night. I saw you with that other girl. I saw your arm around her."

"Asanti calm down. It wasn't…"

She's About That Life: Familiar Territory – Keisha Elle

"I don't want to hear it. Don't explain shit to me."

She hung up before he had a chance to explain. Fuck Jace.

Nothing else needed to be said. He played her young heart.

*****

"I just don't understand what she's doing here!"

Cynthia yelled. Her voice could easily be heard from

Asanti's position on the porch.

"She doesn't have to have a reason to come home.

She's my daughter!" David yelled back.

"Your daughter, hasn't given a damn about any of

us for the last three years. As soon as you start your

campaign for judge, she just all of a sudden comes back

here with her hand out."

"You think this is about money? She hasn't asked

for anything. Honey, she's been through a lot. Cut her some

slack."

She's About That Life: Familiar Territory – Keisha Elle

"So have most of the other people in the world. She gets to run home to daddy for him to save the day. She turned our lives upside down when she was here and I have had it! I can't do it anymore David. I was nice enough to agree to the party, but every time she comes around, she brings her bullshit with her. Our friends and family were here. She caused a scene for nothing."

Komiko's headlights knocked her out of her trance. She had been listening so intently to the loud conversation unfolding inside the house that she didn't realize Komiko had pulled up. Asanti retreated to the car without even telling anyone goodbye.

"Are you okay?" Komiko asked after seeing Asanti's flushed face and glassy eyes.

"I shouldn't have come here."

"Why? What happened?"

She's About That Life: Familiar Territory – Keisha Elle

"I don't even know where to begin. Just know that

Mr. and Mrs. McCoy won't ever have to worry about me,

coming around ever again. And I mean that!" She fastened

her seatbelt and crossed her arms over her chest.

\

Chapter 4

Asanti nervously walked up to the door of Club

Fantasy. After discussing the events that led to her sudden

departure from her father's house with Komiko, Asanti had

a change of heart. She needed money, and fast. According

to Komiko, Club Fantasy was one of the classier places to

entertain men. All of the girls were personally screened and

only the best were allowed to grace the stages. Any girl not

She's About That Life: Familiar Territory – Keisha Elle

worthy of being on the Club Fantasy team was sent packing, just as quickly as she came.

Being comfortable in her own skin gave her the courage to even show up. Although this was all new to her, she was going to shake what her momma gave her – literally. Her whole life revolved around being dependent on someone else. It was time for her to stand on her own two feet. *If you can dance, you can strip right? It's just dancing with your clothes off,* she told herself trying to shake off her nerves.

Pulling the door open, Asanti was immediately stopped by a tall man wearing a black t-shirt with the word SECURITY in big white letters. His overly muscular physique, tattooed arms, and hard expression were intimidating. Asanti stood silent as the man's eyes looked her up and down.

She's About That Life: Familiar Territory – Keisha Elle

"What up Ma?" the man asked with a strong New York accent.

"I'm here for a job," Asanti said, squaring her shoulders, trying to appear tall and confident.

"Go on in," he said, waving her towards another set of doors. "It's slow right now, so somebody will be able to help you."

"Thanks." Asanti smiled and walked through the double doors.

The overwhelming smell of cigarette smoke stopped Asanti in her tracks. The loud smash of the door closing behind her, caused her to look back. The red and white NO SMOKING sign neatly displayed on the back of the door caught Asanti's attention. *The irony,* she thought.

The dimmed lights made it hard to see. Loud music blasted as she scanned the room for an approachable face in

She's About That Life: Familiar Territory – Keisha Elle

the big room. Asanti noticed a well-lit bar with a few patrons on the opposite side of one of the three stages. Her eyes stopped on a girl gracing the only stage being occupied. She couldn't get a clear view of her face because of the lighting, but the way the dark-skinned girl wrapped her thick, shiny legs across the pole and swung around with poise and control reminded her of a well-trained dancer. Her pierced nipples bounced up and down as she twisted and conformed in various acrobatic moves. The loud cheers knocked Asanti out of her trance as the girl abandoned the pole to collect her cash. A big smile appeared on the girl's face as she bent over, with her behind facing a tall, bald gentleman, and allowed him to place two bills inside her G-string. The music was momentarily turned down as a voice captured the attention of the attendees. Asanti's eyes locked on the girl as she remembered her face from the day before.

She's About That Life: Familiar Territory – Keisha Elle

"Give it up for Envy," the male voice said as the girl sauntered her pretty ass off the stage. He smacked her ass lightly as she exited. "Um, um, um... now that's a nice piece of ass right there."

A few whistles and claps erupted as the announcer continued. Asanti stood frozen, taking it all in. *I can do this*, she thought.

Continuing through the club, Asanti walked past several tables with empty chairs and made her way to the bar. She was greeted by an attractive woman not much older than herself. Wearing a black jumpsuit lent to her by Komiko, she was confident that she at least looked the part. The jumpsuit was so tight against her deep curves, that it should have been painted on. A pair of knee-high stiletto boots set the look off. Her hair was pulled back in a slick bun with red, seductive lipstick spread across her lips.

She's About That Life: Familiar Territory – Keisha Elle

"What's your name baby?" the female bartender asked, drying off a shot glass. Her halter top and booty shorts made Asanti feel somewhat overdressed.

"Duchess," she said quickly, letting the nickname given to her by her late grandmother slip off her tongue. The older woman called her mother Julissa, 'Princess', and Asanti was her 'Duchess'. Besides, she did not want to give her real name. Hopefully her dancing stint would be short lived. The less people knew about her, the easier it would be to separate herself when she was ready to bounce.

"Duchess, huh?" the woman asked with a slight smile. She knew that name was fake once it stumbled off Asanti's lips. "Ok, Duchess. Wait a minute." The woman picked up a walkie-talkie off the countertop. She held the button firmly and said, "Rico, there's someone here to see you."

She's About That Life: Familiar Territory – Keisha Elle

Asanti used her index finger to trace the outline of a water ring left by a glass on the bar's surface. She tried to appear disinterested as she listened intently. The conversation was brief and to the point. Asanti heard the male voice on the other end ask, "What she look like Gina? If she looks anything like the last one you sent me tell her we ain't hiring." There was a brief pause as Gina looked Asanti up and down.

"I don't think you'll be disappointed," she said biting her lower lip and winking at Asanti.

Asanti felt uneasy and crossed her arms in front of her. She didn't like the look that Gina gave her. Asanti began contemplating her decision. *Maybe this wasn't a good idea*, she thought as she turned and searched for the exit. She was a few steps away from the door when she heard a male voice behind her.

She's About That Life: Familiar Territory – Keisha Elle

"Aye," the male voice said. "Let me holla at you for a minute."

Asanti turned around as the man caught up with her. He smiled when he noticed that the front of her body was just as appealing as the back. He had emerged from the back of the club when he noticed a perfectly proportioned ass walking towards the door. The businessman in him didn't want money to leave his establishment. The man in him wanted to see what else that body was good for.

"Leaving so soon, pretty lady?" he asked, as he inched his way closer to her.

"I got a busy day tomorrow," Asanti lied.

"On a Saturday?" he asked questioningly.

Asanti tried desperately to think of another lie, but nothing came to mind. She peered down at the floor as she nervously thought about what to say next. She felt a warm hand on her chin, lightly pushing her head up.

"You're too pretty to hold your head down," the man said removing his hand from her chin. "I'm Rico," he continued. "I own the spot."

Asanti gave Rico a shy smile. He appeared to be in his mid-30's. He wasn't overly attractive, but he was far from ugly. The natural twinkle in his dark eyes accented his equally dark skin. His neat dreads were pulled back in a ponytail that rested just below his shoulders. His mustache and goatee were neatly trimmed and his front two teeth had a slight gap.

Asanti looked around and nodded in Rico's direction. "It's a nice place."

She had to admit, the establishment wasn't what she expected. She thought about cracked wood floors and

She's About That Life: Familiar Territory – Keisha Elle

unsecured stripper poles. She remembered seeing a YouTube video of a run-down heavy set stripper. The pole gave out as she swung her big ass around it. The thought made her laugh.

"What's so funny?" Rico asked with a confused look on his face.

"Nothing. I was just thinking about something." Asanti toned down her laugh to a shy smile.

"My office is in the back," Rico said changing the subject. "If it's okay with you, I would like to talk to you a little more about the place."

Asanti looked around again, weighing her options. It was just after noon and the place already had several patrons. They could have easily talked out in the open. She didn't understand why they had to talk in the back when no

She's About That Life: Familiar Territory – Keisha Elle

one would hear them where they stood. Reluctantly, Asanti agreed and followed Rico to his office.

"So, what's your name?" Rico asked as they entered his office. He closed the door behind them and motioned for Asanti to sit down on his white leather couch. The office was cold and clinical. It was a big difference from the inside of the club. Everything in the office was white, from the walls to the floors. Asanti sat back on the comfortable couch and crossed her long legs.

"Duchess," Asanti said examining the room. She was impressed.

"So how long you been dancing?" Rico asked as he took a seat behind his oversized white desk.

"I haven't," Asanti answered truthfully.

Rico raised an eyebrow as he leaned back in his seat.

She's About That Life: Familiar Territory – Keisha Elle

"Are you here for a job?"

"I guess so," Asanti answered in a low tone. She knew she didn't sound convincing, so she added, "I have to start somewhere. I heard Club Fantasy is the place to be seen. I just want a chance." Asanti smiled and bit her bottom lip nervously.

Rico adjusted himself in his seat. He heard what Asanti was saying, but his mind was wondering what she looked like under her jumpsuit.

"So you think you have what it takes?" he asked, changing his focus from her breasts to her eyes. He didn't give her time to respond. He continued, "Stand up."

"What?"

"Stand up," Rico said again walking from his chair to the front of his desk. "Let's see what you're working with."

She's About That Life: Familiar Territory – Keisha Elle

Asanti stood awkwardly, not knowing what to do. She briefly looked at the floor and raised her head to Rico, waiting for a response.

"Turn around," he said admiring the beautiful girl standing before him.

Asanti turned around and placed her hands on her hips. She knew he was checking out her backside and it made her feel self-conscious. She was more than blessed back there, but having a man staring at her made her body tense. Did he like what he saw? What was he thinking?

Silence filled the room. Asanti turned back around and was surprised to see Rico stroking himself through his pants. He licked his lips as he readjusted his semi erect penis and leaned onto the desk.

She's About That Life: Familiar Territory – Keisha Elle

"How old are you, Duchess?" Rico asked, focusing his attention to her lips. He wanted to know if her lips were as soft as they looked.

"Twenty-one," Asanti said, noticing his dark eyes peering at her enticingly.

Not able to calm his growing erection, Rico reached in his pocket and grabbed a wad of twenties wrapped in a rubber band. Asanti's eyes widened.

"I'm gonna try you out. You can audition right now," Rico began. "If I like you, you can start tonight. It's slow right now, but Friday and Saturday nights are money-making nights. I only want the best of the best dancing in my club. Niggas pay good money to see bad bitches putting it down. When a nigga leaves here, he should be satisfied and his pockets should be empty. That is, if you worked hard enough." Rico paused to give Asanti time to absorb

She's About That Life: Familiar Territory – Keisha Elle

what he just said. He continued, "I don't let anybody just come in my spot and work. I personally audition every girl. If I don't like you, my regulars won't like you. I need girls who keep the money coming." Rico looked at Asanti's body from head to toe and removed the rubber band from the money. "Now, let's see what your young ass can do."

Asanti froze. Her eyes grew wide and her cheeks began to flush. She didn't know what to say. She didn't like being put on the spot. Asanti was momentarily stunned as an uptempo beat began to play through speakers that hung in the corners of the ceiling. She didn't notice them before. She wasn't familiar with the song, but she knew how to twerk and the beat was just fast enough. It was either now or never. Taking a deep breath, she began moving her body to the music. Asanti was still uneasy, but she wanted the job. She needed the job. Feeling Rico's eyes burning a hole straight through her, she bounced her ass up and down with more force. The motion off her ass resembled a hard wave crashing back and forth.

"Come on baby," Rico said in his southern drawl. "Show me what you got."

Asanti's pace quickened. She put her hands on her knees and began to dip it low. In her element, she tuned Rico out. She was feeling the music and working up a quick sweat. It was all about her.

Rico couldn't help but notice the way her breasts bounced right along with her ass. His eye for talent told him that Asanti had potential, but closed mouths didn't get fed. She would have to do a lot more in order to make money working for him.

"Take off your clothes," Rico said just above a whisper.

She's About That Life: Familiar Territory – Keisha Elle

Asanti took a deep breath and turned around. She bent over, giving Rico a good view of her ass, and unzipped the back of her boots. She slid each foot out seductively. Not wasting any time, she turned to face him, sliding her arms out of her jumpsuit. Her freed breasts stood at attention in the absence of a bra. Her nervousness and Rico's intense stare instantly hardened her nipples.

Rico sucked his bottom lip as his manhood stood at full attention. Asanti examined his crouch area and exhaled deeply. The thick bulge gracing the front of his pants instantly made her pussy wet.

"We're a nude establishment," Rico began, anticipating the remainder of Asanti's clothes coming off. "Some places only let you see titties, but I feel you should get what you pay for. If you wanna see my girls, you're gonna pay."

She's About That Life: Familiar Territory – Keisha Elle

"Continue," he said in a low tone.

Asanti pulled the jumpsuit down over her stomach and over her wide hips. When the jumpsuit was down around her ankles, she bent down and carefully removed each foot. Kicking it to the side, she stood in front of Rico wearing only a sheer black thong. The growing smile on his face increased her confidence as a new beat began to play through the speakers. She wasn't done just yet. Turning around and putting her full ass on display, she seductively grabbed the sides of her thong and slowly slid them off.

When she turned around, Rico was standing with his dick in his hand. He stroked it, never taking his eyes of her.

"That was nice and all, but we make our own rules around here. I like to think that all my girls have a price. What's yours?"

She's About That Life: Familiar Territory – Keisha Elle

"What are you talking about?"

"For the full package." He stroked his dick again. "You see, happy customers are satisfied customers. Satisfied customers become repeat customers. You might be asked to do a little something extra for the money, if you catch my drift. As long as it puts bodies in those chairs every night, I don't care what you have to do. So once again Ms. Duchess, what is your price?"

"I, I don't know…" Asanti was taken aback by the forwardness of his actions. What was her price? Did she have one? Hell, she didn't know. She wasn't here for the twenty-questions bullshit. She was there for a damn job.

She stood in silence watching Rico's tool grow even bigger. It was so damn erect that when Rico removed his hand, it didn't move. Seeing nine thick inches pointing right in her direction involuntarily made her insides tingle.

She's About That Life: Familiar Territory – Keisha Elle

"How much you got?" Asanti asked, trying to sound confident.

"I like you." Rico smiled his gap toothed smile. "A natural born hustler." Still stroking himself, he continued, "I got a lot of money, and I don't mind sharing, but dancing doesn't pay top dollar around here. We like to explore other talents."

"What kind of talent?"

"Get on your knees," Rico said, all traces of humor gone from his voice. He stood in front of her with money in one hand, and his erect penis in the other.

Asanti did as she was told, lowering her body to the cold, hard floor. She was eye level with his manhood. He removed a few bills from the top of his stack and and threw it in her direction. Green images of Benjamin Franklin hit her knees before falling to the floor.

She's About That Life: Familiar Territory – Keisha Elle

Rico moved closer, position himself toward her mouth. His hard dick grazed her lips. He let out a low groan as pre-cum escaped the head.

Asanti knew what time it was. Either she was going to get up and get dressed, or she was going to make her money. She thought about getting up and hauling her ass out of there as fast as she could, but that would have defeated the purpose. She was there for a job, and if she could come up off a ten minute blow job, it would be time well spent. She licked her lips and let 'Duchess' take control. With little reservation, she let her tongue make a small circle on the tip of his dick, tasting the salty flavor of his pre-cum.

"Do you want a tease, or do you want to release?"

"Release."

She's About That Life: Familiar Territory – Keisha Elle

"You gotta come off more than that. The starting price is five hundred."

"Damn ma, you tryna break the bank?" Rico peeled two more one hundred dollar bills off his stack.

"I'm worth every penny."

She opened wide as she let his rigid shaft penetrate her mouth.

She's About That Life: Familiar Territory – Keisha Elle

She's About That Life: Familiar Territory – Keisha Elle

Chapter 5

Asanti knocked hard on the wood door. After no one appeared, she knocked again. Still nothing. She knocked one last time before placing her ear close to the door in an attempt to hear someone approaching. It was no use. No one was home.

After a pregnant pause, Asanti retreated to her apartment and returned with a small note. She stuffed it under the door. Glancing one last time at the large #3 above the peephole, she walked back across the hall to the comfort of Komiko's condo. She didn't know why her neighbor, whom she had never met, listed apartment #4 as an acceptable drop off for his package. Maybe Komiko knew him, but she wasn't home to take responsibility for someone else's stuff. To make matters worse, the FedEx deliverer didn't even care that she did not know the person

She's About That Life: Familiar Territory – Keisha Elle

listed on the delivery label. Still, Asanti signed the electronic device, taking ownership of JR Water's package.

Closing the door behind her, Asanti threw the package softly on the couch. She retreated to her bedroom and plopped down hard on her king-sized bed. She made herself comfortable and grabbed for the remote. Settling for one of her favorite childhood movies, she prepared herself for another boring night.

It was her first night alone in the furnished two-bedroom apartment. She returned there after the blowup at her father's house. Even though she had spoken to him since leaving, she didn't regret a thing. Asanti told her father that she just needed some space. She didn't want to be a burden. He swore up and down that she could never be one, but Asanti heard the argument. She knew how Cynthia truly felt, and the feeling was mutual. Shawn called several

She's About That Life: Familiar Territory – Keisha Elle

times and after repeatedly sending him to voicemail, he finally left a message.

I came by the condo. I didn't see you. Are you ok? I asked my boy if he knew where you stayed. Call me and let me know everything is okay.

Frustration was evident in his voice. Asanti was glad that when Shawn picked her up for her botched surprise party, she met him outside. He didn't even know which floor she lived on. She would call him when she was ready, and at that moment, she wasn't.

Asanti spent the entire morning helping Komiko pack. She was hired to walk in a fashion show by a local California designer. Meeting him in Atlanta years prior, they developed a business relationship, and he utilized her whenever her could.

She's About That Life: Familiar Territory – Keisha Elle

"You'll do great," Asanti told Komiko, as she zipped up the last of the luggage. It seemed as though she packed her entire closet for the short trip.

"I really hope I do." Komiko arched her back as if she had put in some hard labor. "This can open so many doors for me. A lot of important people will be there."

Asanti stared at the 5'10 beauty. Her long, naturally thin body possessed very few curves – a fashion designer's dream. Her smooth almond skin glistened against her bright yellow romper. Her thick, kinky hair was pulled back in a neat bun, while her dark eyes twinkled in anticipation.

Asanti thought about Komiko as boredom set in. She had been gone for only a few hours, but it already felt like an eternity. She thought about going in to work on her night off, but the drops of rain hitting the windows halted that idea. Accepting that she had a boring life, Asanti

She's About That Life: Familiar Territory – Keisha Elle

focused her attention on the television, until the roles reversed, and the television began watching her.

Three loud knocks echoed off the front door. Asanti flickered her eyes repeatedly trying to come back to reality. Her eyes found the digital clock on her cherry wood night stand. It was 10:30PM. Half asleep and slightly confused, Asanti lazily walked to the door.

"Who is it?" Asanti's voice was deep and hoarse. She cleared her throat. "Who is it?"

Silence.

Looking through the peephole, she could see a big fist coming in her direction. She stepped back instinctively. Another hard series of knocks rattled the door.

"I said who is it?"

"It's me," a deep voice said.

She's About That Life: Familiar Territory – Keisha Elle

"Who's me?"

"Jay."

"You got the wrong apartment." Asanti glanced at the door to ensure it was locked and began to walk back to her bedroom. *The nerve of that guy, knocking on my damn door so late*, Asanti thought to herself. "I guess these Atlanta fools have no respect," she muttered.

"There was a note under my door. Is Komiko here?"

"No. Wait." Asanti remembered leaving the note under the door across the hall. "Just a minute." She grabbed the package off the couch and unlocked the door. When the door opened, her breath caught in her throat. She wasn't expecting Jace Rainwater to be standing on the opposite side of the door. What the hell was going on?

"Asanti," Jace said confused. She was not who he expected to see. "Where's Komiko?"

She's About That Life: Familiar Territory – Keisha Elle

"She's not here right now. I left the note. I didn't realize it was for you. Here's your package." Asanti extended it in Jace's direction.

"Thanks," he said, examining the unopened box. "Komiko would have looked through my shit."

"Well, I'm not Komiko." Asanti kept a straight face, looking Jace up and down. She had to admit, he was still fine as ever. His black fitted slacks and crisp white shirt looked expensive, but to the untrained eye, Asanti couldn't place the designer. The two buttons that were unfastened at the top of his shirt allowed her to peek at his bare chest. *Nice*, she thought to herself, not letting the approval show on her face.

"I'm well aware of that," Jace said running his tongue across his lower lip. "Asanti, can we talk?"

She's About That Life: Familiar Territory – Keisha Elle

"Goodnight," Asanti said dismissing his question. She took one last look at his dark, 6'3 frame. Short, wavy black hair neatly adorned his head. A thin mustache lined his upper lip, while his straight white teeth glistened with every smile. Having him in front of her now brought back a host of bad memories. The person she hated and still loved at the same time was living right next door. Talk about bad luck! Closing the door in his face, she could see the hurt of his bruised ego plastered all across his face.

*****

A couple weeks passed and Asanti was easily settling in to Atlanta life. Club Fantasy had turned her life around for the better. For the first time in her life, she was self-sufficient, and taking care of herself on her own. Although she still lived with Komiko, she held her own weight, splitting all of the bills right down the middle. It felt good knowing that when her bills were paid, she still

She's About That Life: Familiar Territory – Keisha Elle

had enough to play around with. Asanti was happy. Life was good.

Her relationship with Komiko was growing as well. They realized that they had a lot more in common than they previously thought. Komiko didn't meet her own father until she was seven. Initially being told that another man was her father, she learned the truth after her biological father re-entered her mother's life. Komiko valued family and in a short time, she began referring to Asanti as 'Sis.' Their bond became strong - fast. When you saw one, you saw the other. Asanti fit in nicely with Komiko's circle of friends. She even introduced Asanti to some heavy pocket fashion execs. Komiko urged Asanti to make her family a priority. They may have gotten on her nerves, but family was still family. Asanti told her that she would, but honestly, her family was the last thing on her mind.

She's About That Life: Familiar Territory – Keisha Elle

Jace was a different story. She had to admit, he'd matured a lot of the years, both mentally and physically. Every time she heard his keys clinging in the hallway, she would run to the peephole, just to get a look. A couple of times, she just happened to be leaving her apartment at the same time he was arriving. In reality, she began to learn his routine. She would time her exit as soon as she saw his shiny car pull around the corner. He thought it was a coincidence, and she played it off well. Some might have called it stalking, but Asanti didn't care. She received a rush just from being close to him, even though her heart could not fully forgive him. Her body yearned for him, and it was something she couldn't control.

One evening, she noticed a late model BMW pull up to the building. When Jace entered the passenger's side of the car with a duffle bag in hand, the car sped off. Two hours later, the car returned and Jace entered his apartment

She's About That Life: Familiar Territory – Keisha Elle

wearing sweaty gym clothes, still holding the same duffle bag. His hard body appeared as though he lived in the gym, so nothing seemed out of the ordinary. The next night, the same car pulled up, and a beautiful woman wearing a sleek wrap dress and six inch pumps emerged. Jealousy began brewing when Jace opened the door holding a bottle of wine and wearing a wide smile. The fact that the woman was still in his apartment the next morning made her blood boil.

She didn't know why she was becoming infatuated with him all over again. She played him to the left and didn't give him the time of day. Yet, he occupied her dreams more than a little bit. After his face and the things she wanted to do with it made her cum two nights in a row, she finally decided to give in and ask Komiko what the 411 was on Jace Rainwater.

She's About That Life: Familiar Territory – Keisha Elle

"He's cool," Komiko said rubbing lotion on her flawless legs. "Why do you ask?"

"No reason." Asanti hoped her interest wasn't too obvious.

"He told me that you two meet a couple years back right? Through your stepbrother Shawn."

"Yeah. I knew him." Asanti didn't go into detail about how well she knew him. "I lived in Atlanta for my junior and senior years of high school. Jace is my brother's best friend."

"Oh, well, he's single," Komiko said squirting more lotion on her hand and repeating the gesture on the opposite leg. "She looked out the corner of her eye to see Asanti's expression.

"I wasn't…" Asanti began.

She's About That Life: Familiar Territory – Keisha Elle

"Umm hmmm," Komiko said cutting her off. "So you're not interested?"

"Of course not." Asanti turned her nose up to add emphasis to her statement.

She didn't really know if that was a lie or the truth. Somewhere deep inside, her curiosity was peaked. There was just something about Jace. When their paths continued to cross, Asanti took it as a sign. It wasn't out of the ordinary to see your neighbor on a daily basis, but Jace was everywhere. She saw him at the grocery store, movie theater, and even shopping at the mall. It seemed as though the tables had turned and he was now stalking her. When she rolled up in her new black BMW 6-Series, he was the first face she saw.

"Nice," he said with an approving nod. Standing beside his own Range Rover SVR, it wasn't apparent if he was coming or going. "You got good taste." Jace liked Asanti's vibe, even though she dismissed him every time they encountered one another. She was like a complex code that he just couldn't crack.

"Thanks," Asanti said simply. Pressing the lock button on her keyless remote, she gave Jace a half-smile and turned to walk away.

"So, that's it?" Jace asked sincerely.

"What do you mean?"

"You just dismissed me without even giving me a chance."

"A chance for what?"

"To show you what a good guy I am," Jace ran his hand over his 5 o'clock shadow.

She's About That Life: Familiar Territory – Keisha Elle

"You're full of yourself." Asanti walked over and stood directly in front of him. The wind teased the ends of her soft curls as she walked. She opened her mouth to tear in to him for his cockiness, but lost her confidence when she entered his personal space.

"Can I at least take you out?" Jace asked after a moment of awkward silence. He could smell the sweet citrus scent emanating off her sun kissed skin. "You know, show you that I'm not as bad as you make me out to be."

"Why would you do that?" She ignored the stray strands of hair invading her face as the wind picked up. Jace reached up and removed them. The touch alone made Asanti's nipples harden into miniature pearls.

"Because I obviously hurt you. I think that's why you stayed away for so long." His voice was low and serious.

She's About That Life: Familiar Territory – Keisha Elle

Asanti sucked her teeth and rolled her eyes.

"Don't flatter yourself." Her words escaped her lips before she could employ a filter. "You didn't have any control over me leaving. Why don't you go run game on one of your hoes? I don't have time for it."

"I don't have any hoes," Jace said with a boyish grin. "I'm just a single man trying to get to know the beautiful woman in Apartment 704."

Who was this nigga fooling? Asanti thought about calling his ass out right then and there, but she didn't want to show her ass in front of the upscale building. She decided to take a more civil approach.

"I'll let Komiko know." She gave him a wink before turning on her heels.

"So what do I have to do to make you change your mind?" His voice was slightly elevated, making sure that

She's About That Life: Familiar Territory – Keisha Elle

she heard him as she continued to walk away. He watched her intently as the natural sway of her hips gyrated the fabric of her ankle length maxi dress to its own beat. "Damn," he said under his breath.

"I don't know," She kept walking, not missing a beat. "I'm sure you'll think of something."

She's About That Life: Familiar Territory – Keisha Elle

Chapter 6

The music blasted as Asanti spread her legs in a perfect split. She bounced up and down as she shifted her split from left to right. The crowd roared as she carefully untied the sides of her panty bottoms and seductively slid them off. Light beads of sweat poured from her face as she made her way to the ground, lifting both legs behind her head. Her naked body was exposed as the lips of her womanhood glistened for all to see. Cash was thrown on the stage like New Year's Day confetti. Standing up, she gathered her night's earnings and slowly walked off stage, giving the crowd one last view of her perfectly sculpted body.

"You did your thing out there Duchess," Envy said as Asanti reached the back dressing room. She sat facing a vanity mirror putting the finishing touches on her make-up. Her glittered eye shadow and long green wig put her into

She's About That Life: Familiar Territory – Keisha Elle

the character of her 'Seven deadly sins' namesake. "Watching you out there…um…my nipples are still hard."

"Thanks girl," she said shaking her head. She ignored the latter part of Envy's comment and walked over to a set of grey metal lockers. She unlocked the purple combination lock, stuffing her uncounted money inside a black Michael Kors satchel. She quickly closed the locker and plopped down hard, on a white leather couch. She reached over and turned on the floor fan that sat directly in front of her. Closing her eyes, she tried to cool herself off from her high-energy performance.

"Turn that fan off!" a high pitched voice yelled.

Selena and Diana sat at a small card table in the back of the dressing room. As the fan rotated, spurts of air blew in their direction.

She's About That Life: Familiar Territory – Keisha Elle

"I'm sorry Selena," Asanti said in low voice, switching the fan's setting from rotation to stationary.

"Don't apologize to that bitch," Envy chimed in, adding her two cents to the conversation. She smoothed her MAC Myth Tinted Lipgloss over her lips and before lightly blotting it.

"You always got something to say," Selena shot back, pulling a sandwich bag filled with white powder out of her large tan and white Coach tote. "I guess you don't want none of this," she said dangling the bag in the air.

"I didn't say all that," Envy said, as a smile formed on her lips. She slowly stood up, wearing nothing but green pasties over her softening nipples with a small pair of green side-stringed mini shorts. She grabbed a thin, knee length robe from the back of her chair and threw it at Asanti as she

She's About That Life: Familiar Territory – Keisha Elle

made her way to an empty chair at the flimsy card table.
Asanti jumped in her seat as the garment landed in her lap.

Pulling her matching wallet out of her tote, Selena
retrieved her Drivers' License and a one dollar bill.
Emptying some of the contents of the bag onto the table,
she used her Drivers' License to make six neat lines. She
rolled up the bill and used it as a substitute straw. Closing
one of her nostrils with her French-manicured index finger,
she positioned the bill millimeters away from the drug,
sniffed hard, and inhaled a line of coke. She quickly
snorted a second line and firmly pinched her burning nose
with her thumb and index finger. Passing the rolled up bill
to Envy, she mimicked Selena's gesture as she quickly took
her two lines like a champ.

She's About That Life: Familiar Territory – Keisha Elle

Envy extended the bill across the table to Diana. She smiled as the familiar euphoric feeling crept upon her. Diana shook her head and held up her hand in protest.

"I can't," Diana said, breaking her silence. She had been quiet the entire evening, only speaking when spoken to.

"Why not?" Envy asked curiously.

Diana's quiet demeanor was out of character. From the solemn expression on her face, Envy could tell something was wrong.

"I'm pregnant," Diana mumbled, just above a whisper.

"What else is new?" Envy asked with a straight face.

She's About That Life: Familiar Territory – Keisha Elle

Diana rolled her eyes, looking in Envy's direction. Her shoulder length bleach blonde hair revealed dark roots. Her thin nose scrunched up as her pale White skin flushed crimson. She crossed her arms over her small breasts and gave Envy the evil eye.

"What's that supposed to mean?" she scoffed.

"You're pregnant every other month," Envy began. She wasn't trying to be harsh, but sometimes, the truth hurts. "You're at the clinic so much they know you by name. I don't know why you just don't get on some type of birth control. Better yet, stop letting that nigga Rodney run up in you raw."

"Tell us how you really feel," Asanti said joining the conversation. She sat down at the only available seat left at the table. She crossed her long legs and adjusted the robe, tucking her breasts back in their proper place.

She's About That Life: Familiar Territory – Keisha Elle

"See, I never have that problem." Envy watched Asanti closely while she readjusted the robe. "Nothing goes up in me except a stiff tongue or a dildo. Believe me, I learned that lesson a long time ago." Envy thought about the embarrassment of going to the clinic and finding out she had two sexually transmitted infections. It happened over five years ago, but she had sworn off men ever since.

"And she would rather it be the stiff tongue," Selena spoke up, adding her opinion to the conversation.

There was no shame in Envy's game. She made no secret about her attraction towards the same sex. The joy of watching a woman between her legs turned her on more than any man ever could.

"Damn right!"

She's About That Life: Familiar Territory – Keisha Elle

Selena stood up and extended her hand. Envy smiled, stood up, and slapped Selena's open hand, giving her a high five.

"I know that's right girl!" Selena returned to her sitting position.

"You too?" Asanti asked puzzled,

"I'm just having fun." Selena ran her fingers through her hair. "I like to cum. I don't care if it's a man or woman that gets me there."

"Here," Envy said to Asanti, as she motioned the rolled up bill in Asanti's direction. She turned her attention back to Diana and continued, "You know I love you D."

"Whatever," Diana said rolling her eyes.

Asanti looked at the setup in front of her. She began to unroll the bill, rendering its previous purpose useless.

She's About That Life: Familiar Territory – Keisha Elle

"What the fuck are you doing?!" Selena asked, yelling at the same time. She stood up and swiped the bill out of Asanti's hand in one quick motion. Rolling the bill back up, she quickly took another hit.

Asanti looked on with wide eyes. Selena was the epitome of beauty. Her long black hair and dark almond shaped eyes matched her sun kissed skin. The slight accent that left her bilingual tongue was almost as seductive as her round, shapely Puerto Rican ass. Even sniffing powder, she was a sight to be seen.

"Go ahead," Selena said wiping the excess powder from her nose.

Asanti looked down at the last lone hit still spread out on the table in front of Selena. Her heart began to race as she felt the burn of three pair of eyes on her. Other than satisfying her curiosity once with a joint, Asanti never tried

She's About That Life: Familiar Territory – Keisha Elle

anything else. When the opportunity presented itself, Asanti would think of the way drugs negatively impacted her mother's life. It was easy to resist, like the D.A.R.E motto preached. Today was different. Her curiosity was peaked as she looked at the calm and peaceful look that took over Envy and Selena's faces. She too wanted that feeling. She had a long night of mingling and ass shaking ahead of her. Feeling the effects of long nights, and very little sleep, her young body was running on empty. She needed a happy medium in order to continue. The temptation in front of her would be just that.

Taking the rolled up bill from Selena's loose fingers, she stood up, and stood directly over the lone line. She bent down, closed one of her nostrils with her index finger, positioned the homemade straw directly above the line, and inhaled hard and quick. The immediate burn of the

She's About That Life: Familiar Territory – Keisha Elle

foreign substance tingled her nose, causing her eyes to water.

"Damn," Asanti said, immediately grabbing her nose.

"You'll be okay, lightweight," Envy snickered as she stood up from the table. "It only burns for a second."

Asanti opened her mouth to respond, but an unfamiliar feeling crept upon her. She felt a weird drainage in the back of her throat. She tasted the nasty mixture as she sluggishly swallowed it down. The feeling in her throat slowly subsided, only to be replaced by numbness. Her body immediately felt relaxed as her pupils slowly began to dilate. She didn't have a care in the world.

"You want another hit?" Selena asked, pointing to the open bag on the table.

She's About That Life: Familiar Territory – Keisha Elle

"Yeah, I'll take another one," Asanti replied without hesitation.

"I would love to stay and chat with you bitches, but I got money to make," Envy chimed in, adjusting her ass cheeks in her shorts. Glancing at the large clock gracing the dull gray wall, she continued. "Come on Diana, we up next."

Diana and Envy exited the room as Asanti and Selena both took two more hits. Selena schooled Asanti on using different nostrils. She advised her that using the same nostril increased the numbness, and that was not a good feeling. Asanti absorbed the information like a sponge as she learned more and more about her new friend – coke.

The dressing room door swung open and three loud bitches walked in. Asanti and Selena turned to each other, shaking their heads in unison. They knew what time it was.

She's About That Life: Familiar Territory – Keisha Elle

Getting up from the table, Asanti waited for Selena to secure her private possessions in her locker. The two walked out together leaving the loud mouth females to talk amongst themselves.

The pair walked the long hallway to the main room and stopped before reaching the bar. An overwhelming smell of marijuana mixed with sweat filled the air. They gave each other a quick nod and a smile as they made their way to opposite sides of the room.

Two girls gyrated on opposite stages as a third girl exited the large stage in the middle. Asanti slowly walked past the row of stages as she sought out a potential high roller for the night. Asanti stopped abruptly as a hand forcefully grabbed the back of her ass. Turning around with much attitude, Asanti brought her hand up for a quick slap. She halted when she realized who it was.

She's About That Life: Familiar Territory – Keisha Elle

"Oh!" Asanti said nervously. Her face began to flush. She lowered her hand as two red blotches appeared on her cheek. "I didn't know it was you. You almost got slapped."

"I'm glad you didn't," Rico said smiling, stepping closer. "I need to holla at you for a minute."

"Ok." Asanti smiled nervously. Her heart was pumping hard in her chest. "Do you want to do it now? I got a couple of minutes before my next set."

A loud familiar tune blasted through the speakers, capturing Asanti's attention. She smiled, watching her friends seductively make their entrance. Envy's skin glistened as she sashayed her wide hips on the stage, immediately grabbing the pole in the center. Diana slowly walked out of Envy's shadow and cupped her perky breasts from behind. A wave of attendees deserted their tables and

She's About That Life: Familiar Territory – Keisha Elle

found their way closer to the stage. A crowd formed around the soft porn scene as single bills began to rain on the stage.

Rico glanced at Envy as her head slowly fell back in enjoyment. He remembered the day he hired her four year prior. It was the same day she took all nine inches of his rock hard dick straight up the ass. She fingered herself while he pounded her glory hole for fifteen minutes straight. When he was ready to nut, he pulled out quickly, allowing Envy to suck him the rest of the way off. Her warm mouth was the icing on the cake, causing him to shake involuntarily and cum in her mouth. He coated her throat with his warm semen. Envy swallowed every drop. Now, all that good mouth action was playing for the other team. Rico turned away, feeling the familiar tingle indicating the beginning of a hard-on.

She's About That Life: Familiar Territory – Keisha Elle

"Let's do it now," Rico grabbed Asanti's hand. "We can go to my office."

Asanti placed her hand in Rico's as they made their way through the crowd of people. They entered Rico's office and he closed and locked the door behind them.

Asanti stood in the middle of the room, wondering what the hell Rico needed to talk to her about. She was still considered new to the club, but she was fitting in nicely. Her 'one night only' had turned into six full weeks of dancing. The money was just too good to pass up. Word of mouth spread quickly and after a couple days, men and women both formed lines outside of Club Fantasy just to see the big booty exotic chick that everyone was talking about.

She's About That Life: Familiar Territory – Keisha Elle

"So, what do you want to talk to me about?" Asanti asked, breaking the awkward silence that formed between them.

"I just want to see how everything is going." Rico took a seat on his white leather couch. He patted the space directly beside him, gesturing for Asanti to sit down.

"Everything's fine." Asanti filled the space beside him. She crossed her long legs and repositioned her robe to cover her assets underneath.

"Are the girls treating you right?" His eyes skimmed down the length of Asanti's legs.

"Yeah, they're cool." She didn't know where Rico was going with his questioning.

"Do you need anything...from me?" Rico said with a slick smile.

She's About That Life: Familiar Territory – Keisha Elle

"No. I don't think so."

"Are you sure?" Rico's voice was low and breathy.

She studied him for a second. Every time she hit the stage, his eyes were on her. She noticed his not so subtle stares weeks ago. The place could be on fire and his gaze would not leave her until she was out of sight. Everywhere she turned, he was there. There was no way it was a coincidence.

"Rico," Asanti began in low tone, "I know you called me in here for a reason, and it's not to see how I'm doing. What do you really want?"

"You."

No man had ever been so direct with her. She didn't know what to say, but in a weird way, she liked it.

She's About That Life: Familiar Territory – Keisha Elle

"I...I..." Asanti tried to find the right words, but nothing came to mind.

"You don't have to say anything," Rico said cutting her off. "Just let me..."

"I have a boyfriend!" Asanti blurted out before she could catch herself. It was a lie, but the fire Rico was igniting inside her both scared her and turned her on at the same damn time.

"You have a boyfriend?"

"Yes, he's..."

"Irrelevant." Rico finished her sentence.

Rico placed his hand on Asanti's thigh and slowly moved it up. Her breathing quickened as his hand found the space where her thighs crossed one over the other. Nudging it softly with his fingers, Asanti uncrossed her legs,

She's About That Life: Familiar Territory – Keisha Elle

allowing Rico to freely roam in between her legs. Moving in closer, he untied her robe, allowing it to fall open.

His fingers found her entrance. Subconsciously holding his breath, he inserted a thick finger deep within her and quickly withdrew it. Her warm, natural juices coated his finger. He inserted another finger and slowly dug in and out of her while using his thumb to massage her clit.

Asanti closed her eyes, enjoying the feel of Rico's touch. She arched her back as his lips found one of her erect nipples. His tongue danced around the circumference of her nipple. Within seconds, she was wet. She took control over massaging her clit as Rico inserted a third finger and switched to the other breast.

Releasing her breast from his mouth, Rico dropped to his knees and buried his face into her pussy. Using slow, circular strokes, he gently massaged her clit with his

She's About That Life: Familiar Territory – Keisha Elle

tongue. Asanti gripped his head, tangling her fingers in his dreads. She rocked her hips to his rhythm as he returned three fingers inside her dripping love box. He sucked her swollen clit. Asanti widened her legs and pushed his face deeper into her hot spot. The explosive force on the verge of being released came to an abrupt end when three loud knocks echoed off the door. Rico sat up quickly, his face full of Asanti's glistening juices. Asanti's eyes shot open, as surprise and frustration hit her at the same time.

"Who is it?" Rico called out. He placed his hand lightly across her stomach, preventing her from sitting up.

"Ah, yo Boss Man," a deep baritone voice said. "We got a situation out here. These niggas are fighting and throwing bottles and shit."

Rico shook his head and turned back to Asanti. He was so close to turning her out and laying some serious pipe on her young ass. The hoodlums acting a fool in his club had fucked up his plans. He really needed to bust a nut. The smell of Asanti was still in the air, stiffening his throbbing wood. He could still taste her sweet nectar on his tongue.

"Handle that shit Big D," Rico said hoarsely. "I'll be out in a minute."

Rico stood to his feet with his dick hard in his pants. Without saying a word, he used his hand to wipe the remnants of Asanti's pussy off his lips and headed towards the door. Opening it, he took two steps out before stopping. He turned in Asanti's direction.

"Raincheck baby." He closed the door behind him.

Asanti fumbled with her robe and loosely tied it in annoyance. The feeling of being so close, but not close enough infuriated her. The high that she previously felt was

She's About That Life: Familiar Territory – Keisha Elle

gone and was replaced by raging female hormones. *"Why did he have to interrupt us? He could have handled that shit on his own,"* she thought to herself. Standing to her feet, she jumped as the opening door startled her. Rico stood in the doorway with a sly grin on his face.

"Do me a favor," he said, leaning into the room.

"What's that?" Asanti asked, tying her robe tighter.

"Tell yo nigga I said what's up."

She's About That Life: Familiar Territory – Keisha Elle

Chapter 7

Hey, it's me. I'm breathing, so that means I'm still

alive. Sorry I didn't return your call sooner. I got your

voicemail. I'll talk to you soon. Love you.

Asanti swiped the end call icon on her large

screened phone.

She applied a thin layer of lip gloss over her lips.

Her straightened hair was pulled into a high bun. Her oiled

skin shimmered under her black lace mini dress. Tonight

was going to be a great night. She stepped back and gave

herself a once over in her full-length mirror. She was as

close to perfection as she could get, and she knew it.

The silenced cell phone began to vibrate and light

up in various colors in front of her. She answered the call

without paying attention to the name or number. She knew

who it was.

She's About That Life: Familiar Territory – Keisha Elle

"Hey, Shawn," Asanti grabbed her purse and scanned the room to make sure she wasn't forgetting anything.

"So you do know how to return a call?" Sarcasm was evident in his voice, even though she could tell he was pissed off. "You haven't been to the house in weeks. You're ignoring your David. You're sending me to voicemail. What's up?"

"I just needed some time to myself, that's all." Asanti sighed, not ready to answer Shawn's fifty million questions. Right now, she just wanted her brother to know that she was okay, not make her feel like she was a contestant on Jeopardy.

"Time to yourself? What for?"

"Do I have to have a reason? I am a grown woman."

"Oh you're grown now?"

She's About That Life: Familiar Territory – Keisha Elle

"Why are you repeating everything I say? I just needed some me time. Is that too much to ask?"

"I just don't understand. No one has heard from you in weeks and all you have to say is you needed some me time. You haven't been to the house to see Kat. She's due any day now and David has me as the middle man trying to get a hold of you. Everybody's worried about you sis," Shawn rambled on all in one breath.

"Well, you can tell everyone not to worry. I'm fine." Asanti said, taking the elevator to the ground floor. Komiko was dressed and waiting for her in her car.

"We'll talk tonight," Shawn said matter-of-factly.

"No, we won't." Asanti was getting frustrated. Reaching Komiko's passenger side door, she slid her small frame into the seat and closed the door. She continued, "I gotta go. I'll call you tomorrow. I promise. Love you."

Before Shawn could interject, Asanti ended the call.

She's About That Life: Familiar Territory – Keisha Elle

"Is everything okay?" Komiko asked, maneuvering her luxury car onto the road.

"Yeah, it's just Shawn. I took your advice and called him. Now she wants to know everything." Asanti sighed.

"Well, what did you expect?"

Asanti didn't answer. Instead, she watched the lights of the passing cars bounce off her passenger's side window. She missed Shawn. It was great hearing his voice. When they were younger, they were inseparable. Even though they didn't resemble at all, people thought that they were blood related because of their close relationship. Shawn was the type of big brother that ever girl wished she had. He was big and strong, but gentle and compassionate when it came to Asanti. He warned her about the knuckleheads in the street, and stressed the importance of

She's About That Life: Familiar Territory – Keisha Elle

valuing herself; mind, body, and spirit. If she didn't do it, a man sure as hell wouldn't.

"Snap out of it!" Komiko noticed Asanti's blank expression. "We're going to have some fun tonight." Briefly taking her eyes off the road, she smiled at her friend.

Komiko was invited to a local industry party. All the big names in Atlanta were expected to be there. Komiko knew most of the likely attendees personally, and she never missed an opportunity to network herself. She invited Asanti as her plus one. She knew that opportunities arose when you surrounded yourself with the right people.

Asanti immediately felt uneasy when they pulled onto the dark street. Abandoned buildings with boards covering the broken windows could be seen on both sides of the street. Grabbing her clutch purse tighter, Asanti felt apprehensive about getting out of the car. Using her index

She's About That Life: Familiar Territory – Keisha Elle

finger, she pushed the lock button. All the doors locked in unison. She was in the hood and didn't want to take any chances.

"What's wrong?" Komiko asked, circling her car around a full parking lot. The lot was filled to capacity. She noticed a booth with a sign displaying the word VALET. She immediately turned her car in its direction.

"I was expecting something else." Asanti looked over her shoulder. She hadn't felt this paranoid since leaving Louisville.

"It looks better inside. It's been renovated. An investment firm just purchased this whole block. They're fixing these buildings up." Komiko pointed to the building housing the party. "That one has already been renovated. Just wait until we get inside, you'll be amazed."

Komiko handed her keys to the eager valet attendant after stepping out of the car. Her red and black

She's About That Life: Familiar Territory – Keisha Elle

Donna Karan tube dress sparkled against her almond skin. She walked confidently in her five-inch black heels. A pair of ruby studded earrings graced her ears, while a dozen diamond studded bangles hung loosely on her small wrist. She led the way as Asanti followed closely behind.

A line of patrons waiting to enter the building wrapped halfway around the block. Komiko walked up to the door, gave the bald, muscular security guard one of her million dollar smiles, and the two were let in without waiting.

Allowing Komiko to lead, Asanti followed behind absorbing the scene. Bright lights flickered and danced off the huge, loft-style room. A DJ booth sat overlooking the crowd below.

Asanti's gaze turned to a tall bronze-toned woman with a pair of DDD breasts almost spilling out of her low cut, tight dress. The jumping lights made her sequined

She's About That Life: Familiar Territory – Keisha Elle

dress sparkle.

"That's Raven," Komiko said, noticing Asanti's stare. "She works at the same law firm as Jace."

Asanti's gaze turned into an all-out stare. The woman had on the highest pair of heels she had ever seen. They had to be over six inches. Her contorted feet looked uncomfortable, stuffed in the small shoe.

"She doesn't look like a lawyer."

"Tell me about it. She has a problem with anyone who gets close to Jace. She acts like that's her man or something. She's pathetic." Komiko rolled her eyes and displayed a closed-lip smile. Scanning the room to ensure no one was close enough to hear her, she continued, "She should have bought an ass to match those huge tits."

Asanti laughed loudly, causing several party goers to look her way. Embarrassed, she lowered her head. Komiko looped her arm around Asanti's and began

She's About That Life: Familiar Territory – Keisha Elle

walking. Giggling like school girls, their minds were momentarily preoccupied.

"She looks familiar for some reason." Asanti couldn't place where, but she never forgot a face. She had seen Raven before.

"It definitely wasn't the club. Poor thang's ass is as flat as two pancakes." Komiko clapped her hands together to emphasize the point.

Asanti erupted in laughter, not caring about the scene she was making. Komiko soon followed.

"What's so funny?" a familiar voice asked, startling the girls.

Asanti and Komiko turned around to see Jace holding two champagne flutes. He extended a drink to both girls, which they graciously accepted.

"Hey Jace!" Komiko transferred her drink from her right hand to her left as she reached up and hugged Jace tightly. She gave him a soft kiss on his cheek.

Jace stared in Asanti's direction. She was wearing the hell out of her dress. After a pregnant pause, he finally, smiled that boyish grin that Asanti used to love so much. When he spoke, his voice was like music to her ears.

"What's up Asanti? I'm glad you could make it."

Asanti felt another pair of eyes on her. She noticed Raven, intently watching their exchange. Asanti saw the familiar ping of jealousy spread across her face. It was time for Asanti to act a damn fool. Mimicking Komiko, Asanti wrapped her free hand around Jace's waist and gave him a tight hug.

"Thanks for the drink." Asanti took a small sip from the glass.

"You're welcome."

Jace was happy she was being cordial. Asanti was unpredictable at times, but he knew he would eventually wear he down. He didn't know it would happen so soon. Watching her walk into the door, he immediately noticed the way her lace dress hugged her body tightly. Holding out as long as he could, he brought over the champagne just to be close to her.

"Thanks for inviting us," Komiko began, filling the awkward silence. Komiko winked in at Asanti. She hadn't told her that Jace was the one who invited them to the party.

"No problem. There's actually someone I would like you to meet. One of my frat brothers is looking for a couple models for a fashion show he's putting together. I put your name out there. He would like to meet you." Jace spoke, but his eyes remained on Asanti. Her fierce curves had him in a trance. "We have a table in the back if you two want to join us."

She's About That Life: Familiar Territory – Keisha Elle

"What do you think?! Of course I do!" Komiko answered without hesitation. Tugging on her reluctant friend's arm, she gave Asanti a reassuring smile. "Lead the way."

The trio walked silently through the crowd. Asanti could not help feeling that she was being watched. Looking around nervously, she locked eyes with Raven. She didn't know why the girl was staring at her. Pulling the front of her mini-dress down, she continued her stride. They stopped in front of a circular table with two of the eight cushioned chairs already occupied by Shawn and Kat. They stopped and looked up when Jace approached.

"Oh my God! Asanti! I haven't seen you in forever." Kat stood up quickly, waddling her overly pregnant frane over to Asanti. Her long, blonde hair hung almost to her waist. She hugged Asanti tightly, truly happy to see her.

She's About That Life: Familiar Territory – Keisha Elle

Kat was Shawn's longtime girlfriend. They had been inseparable since meeting at a party during their freshmen year. Kat, or Katrina – as her government ID would say, was taking Undergraduate classes at Georgia State University while Shawn focused on Pre-Law at Emory University. They kept their relationship quiet for a long time out of fear of her family's disapproval. She was surprised when she brought her Black boyfriend to her All-White Thanksgiving dinner, and her mother accepted him with open arms. It took a little bit more convincing on her dad's part. Thanks to Sunday football and their love of the Atlanta Falcons, the men bonded, and the rest was history.

Asanti released the embraced and stepped back. She felt Kat's hard stomach during their hug. She looked as if she was carrying a basketball under her floor length, light blue maternity dress, which almost perfectly matched her baby blue eyes. She was one of the lucky ones, only

She's About That Life: Familiar Territory – Keisha Elle

gaining weight in her mid-section. Everything else was as tight and perfect as it once was.

Asanti placed her hands on Kat's stomach. Kat placed her pale hands on top of Asanti's and pushed inward.

"Do you feel that?"

Asanti's eyes widened when she felt an undeniable kick, or maybe even a punch from inside Kat's stomach.

"Oh my." Kat grabbed her stomach. "This is the most active he's been all day."

"He was waiting for his aunty," Asanti said in a baby voice.

"I'm glad he didn't have to wait too long." Shawn appeared behind her. With all of the commotion over the baby, she didn't realize that he had stood up.

"Hi Shawn." Asanti hugged her brother, now realizing what he meant when he said he would see her

She's About That Life: Familiar Territory – Keisha Elle

later. He knew she would be there. "We'll talk later," she whispered in his ear, not wanting to release the embrace.

"Ok." He didn't object. Shawn was never the one to cause a scene in public. "You look beautiful by the way."

Jace loosely grabbed Komiko's arm, gaining her attention. She was so focused on Asanti and Shawn that she hadn't noticed the well-dressed man walking in their direction. Jace extended his arm, palm side up, in the man's direction.

"Komiko, this is Carlos Santana, the designer I was telling you about."

"It's nice to meet you." Komiko extended her hand to the man. He grabbed it gently, bringing it to his mouth for a soft kiss. He lifted her hand high, twirling her around so he could see all of her.

"The pleasure is all mine. She's exactly what we're looking for. She's perfect."

She's About That Life: Familiar Territory – Keisha Elle

A pair of arms wrapped around Komiko from behind swiftly, momentarily ending the the exchange. Asanti didn't know whether to swing or not react at all. A male's body pushed up behind Komiko so close that they should have been conjoined. Confusion crept upon her face as Rico tightened his grip, and began planting soft kisses along the nape of Komiko's neck.

What the hell? Asanti thought to herself. Rico and Komiko? Asanti had no idea.

Komiko giggled like a school girl, turning around to kiss Rico on his lips. He whispered in her ear. She excused herself before walking in the direction of the open bar.

Jace gave Rico a sly grin and embraced his boy. Although they didn't see each other on a daily basis, there was no love lost.

She's About That Life: Familiar Territory – Keisha Elle

"It's good seeing you, Jay. My schedule's been so fucking busy. This is the first night I've been able to get out."

"It's all good. You're here now." Jace stepped closer to Asanti, laying claim to her. He could see Rico's eyes tracing the lace hem of her short dress. Jace peeped the situation. He knew how his friend operated. He didn't want Rico to think that Asanti was free reign. Looking at Asanti, he opened his mouth to speak once again. "This is..."

"I already know. We've met." Rico cut Jace off before he finished the introduction. His deceptive eyes lowered into slants before rising up Asanti's dress and eventually locking with hers. Asanti stood frozen. She didn't know why, but she hoped his ass wouldn't blurt out that he had her on her knees or that she worked for him for that matter. If she knew Komiko was was with him, she

would have never crossed that line.

"How you two know each other?" Jace asked,

confused.

"Komiko," Rico blurted out reading the 'please

don't say anything' expression on Asanti's face.

"Did someone call my name?" Komiko appeared

holding a small glass of brown liquor. She passed it to

Rico.

"I need some air. Excuse me." Asanti turned around

and began walking.

"What's wrong?" Komiko asked, grabbing for

Asanti's arm. She couldn't figure out why Asanti's mood

suddenly shifted. She turned to Jace.

"Did you say something to her?"

"He didn't say anything to me." Asanti interrupted,

trying to de-escalate the situation. She was still in ear shot,

She's About That Life: Familiar Territory – Keisha Elle

trying to remember the direction of the exit. "I just need some fresh air. I'll be back."

Asanti started her stride towards the door once again. She drowned out the noise around her. She didn't want to lose focus. Dodging tables and small crowds of people, she found the exit and calmly stepped out.

The cool air felt good on her skin. Throwing her head back, she welcomed the steady breeze. Closing her eyes, she took deep breaths. A calmness crept over her body, allowing her to relax.

"It looks like you need one of these," a soft voice said, extending a teal and white cigarette box in Asanti's direction.

"No thank you." Asanti snapped out of her peaceful trance to see Raven standing beside her. "I don't smoke."

"Suite yourself." Raven shrugged and took a deep pull of her already lit cigarette.

She's About That Life: Familiar Territory – Keisha Elle

The two women stood there awkwardly, each not knowing what to say. Asanti was puzzled, not knowing why Raven was invading her space. Raven broke the silence.

"I'm Raven and you are?"

Asanti didn't answer. Instead, she stared off in the distance.

"I go to these parties all the time, but I've never seen you before. Do you come to these events often?"

Realizing that Raven was not going to shut up, Asanti answered the question.

"No, this is my first time." Suddenly the breeze became cool and Asanti rubbed her arms trying to warm herself up.

"Do you have a jacket? I have one inside?" Raven tried the friendly approach.

"No, I'm fine. I'll be going in shortly."

She's About That Life: Familiar Territory – Keisha Elle

"So, you're Komiko's girl?" Raven asked, blowing smoke out of her mouth as she spoke. Her deep red lipstick left a ring around the filter of her cigarette.

"Yeah, she's a good friend." Asanti was short with Raven's meddling ass. She was trying not to give too much away. She really didn't know what Raven wanted. Peeping the slick eye roll and fake smile, she was almost certain that this girl had an ulterior motive. Asanti was not going to be the one to fill her curiosity.

"She's a nice girl…Very talented…" The sarcasm was evident in her voice. Her compliments were as fake as her DDD titties standing at attention.

Asanti knew what time it was. This girl was phishing for information. Asanti just didn't understand why. She decided to end the conversation.

She's About That Life: Familiar Territory – Keisha Elle

"Enjoy the rest of your evening." She headed in the direction of the door. If she didn't return soon, she knew Komiko would get worried and come look for her.

"You too, Asanti. I'm sure we'll be seeing a lot of each other."

Asanti stopped mid stride and spun around. *How the hell does she know my name?* she thought. Before any words could escape her mouth, she saw Raven walking confidently in the opposite direction.

Chapter 8

Asanti stood like a statue under the flickering lights.

She waited patiently, ready to walk out on stage. The DJ

introduced her to the crowd. Her preferred, fast pace, hip

hop beat was noticeably absent. Tonight was different. The

beat started as Ginuwine's voice blared through the

speakers. Asanti took slow steps toward the center of the

stage. Her long hair hung straight down her back. A short

pink silk robe was tied loosely at her waist. Her long legs

glistened with honey bronze shimmer lotion.

Envy followed behind wearing a matching robe.

Her usually loud, colorful wig was replaced by a shoulder-

156

She's About That Life: Familiar Territory – Keisha Elle

length black bob. Asanti moved her body slowly to the music. Envy copied her movements. The pair began their walk towards the edge of the stage. They passed the secured pole in the center of the stage and began their choreographed routine. Asanti took the lead, outshining Envy, taking her seductive moves to the floor. She was on all fours, gyrating her hips, slow and steady. Envy stepped over her, lowering herself onto Asanti's lower back.

The feel of Envy's warm body touching hers excited Asanti. She wasn't into women, but the hot, sweaty atmosphere, combined with the lack of sex, put her in the mood. She wasn't acting anymore. Instead, she enjoyed Envy's thick thighs squeezing against her small waist and Envy's heated middle grinding her back.

Envy opened her robe and let it fall down her shoulders before eventually falling to the floor. Envy

She's About That Life: Familiar Territory – Keisha Elle

reached back, finding the hem of Asanti's robe. She pulled

it up, exposing Asanti's bare ass for all to see. Her hairless

opening peeked through the small gap between her thighs.

Envy took advantage of the situation, slowly rubbing the

smooth entrance and allowing her index finger to slide its

way through. Asanti closed her eyes and let out of soft

moan. Her eager body gladly accepted. The motion of

Envy's fingers slowly moving in and out caused Asanti to

arch her back as another moan escaped her lips.

The packed crowd went wild. Money began pouring

on the stage. It seemed as though everyone migrated from

their tables to stand close to the stage. Hands attempted to

get a quick feel of the sex scene taking place before them.

Two muscular hands appeared out of nowhere and

controlled the situation. Although security intervened

quickly, more chaos was brewing. A fight broke out when a

She's About That Life: Familiar Territory – Keisha Elle

trampled man reached his feet and began swinging on everyone within reach. A huge brawl ensued.

Envy an Asanti seemed oblivious to the scene playing out just below the stage. When a bottle flew through the air and shattered on the stage, they both jumped to their feet, nearly missing the shattering glass. The two retreated behind the dark curtain and exited the stage. They didn't stop as their night's earnings were being stuffed into a few greedy pockets.

"What the fuck is going on?" Selena questioned, watching Envy and Asanti run into the dressing room. They slammed the door behind them. The pair looked as if they had just seen a ghost.

"Girl….," Envy began. She was clearly out of breath. "We were just getting into our set and the next thing I know a bottle comes flying on the stage. When I looked

She's About That Life: Familiar Territory – Keisha Elle

up, all I saw were fists swinging. We got our asses up out of there fast!"

"What?" Diana let go of her flimsy bra top. Her feet moved to the speed of lightning, headed toward the door. Selena stepped forward and blocked her exit.

"Where the hell are you going?"

"I just want to make sure Rico, I mean, everything's okay?"

Asanti gave her a hard side eye. She was just about to question her slip of the tongue, but Selena cut her off.

"What is your pregnant ass going to do? Hunh? What are you going to do?"

"I don't know, I…" A queasy feeling came over Diana. She turned around, her eyes searching for something to catch the contents of her stomach that were creeping upward. Without warning, she covered her mouth as her liquefied dinner oozed through her fingers and splattered to the floor.

"Look at you." Selena shook her head in disgust. "I'm sure your baby daddy has everything under control." She emphasized the words baby daddy with an eye roll. "Now clean that shit up!"

"Did I miss something?" Asanti grabbed a towel sitting across the back of a chair. She handed it to Diana.

"Selena has a big mouth." Diana wiped the leftover vomit off her face and hands. She then turned her attention to the mess on the floor.

"You're pregnant by Rico?" Asanti's eyes widened. She lifted her hand to her mouth in surprise.

The door swung open, startling the four girls. Rico stuck his head in and surveyed the scene.

She's About That Life: Familiar Territory – Keisha Elle

"Is everything okay in here?" he asked, his voice filled with frustration.

"We're good boss," Envy spoke up.

"Is everything okay out there?" Diana asked, genuinely concerned.

Rico gave her one of his "Shut the fuck up looks.'

"It's fine. I handled it." His voice was cold. "Get your shit on. You're up next."

"Rico, I…." The door slammed shut before Diana could finish her statement.

Diana stood expressionless. Rico had disrespected her a lot behind closed doors, but never had he done it in front of anyone. Even though she was embarrassed, his actions didn't surprise her.

She's About That Life: Familiar Territory – Keisha Elle

"Are you okay?" Asanti asked, placing her hand on Diana's shoulders.

"I'm fine. I just need a minute." Diana wiped the tears trickling down her face. She gave a weak smile before rushing off to the bathroom.

"I'll check on her." Selena said, following her friend.

Asanti and Envy stood in awkward silence. For the first time since meeting her, Asanti did not know what to say. Envy picked up on her hesitation and spoke first.

"I just want you to know that what happened up there...on stage...that was just business."

"What are you talking about?"

"You know...what happened up there. Look, you're a pretty girl and..."

She's About That Life: Familiar Territory – Keisha Elle

"Don't let it happen again!" Asanti barked. "I am strictly dickly."

"I couldn't tell," Envy smirked. She could see Asanti's face flush with embarrassment. "I was just giving the crowd what they wanted. Men love seeing girl on girl action. It's not my fault you enjoyed it."

Asanti swallowed hard, knowing that what Envy said was true. She actually enjoyed the feel of Envy's fingers exploring her most intimate area. Although when she closed her eyes and envisioned her treasure chest being caressed, she never thought it would be Envy's skilled fingers putting in the work. Seeing the confident smirk on Envy's face rubbed Asanti the wrong way.

"Enjoyment and work are two different things. This is my job." Asanti raised her index finger close to Envy's face. "Do not, I repeat, do not let it happen again."

She's About That Life: Familiar Territory – Keisha Elle

Walking over to her locker, Asanti opened it and retrieved her things. She quickly dressed back into the t-shirt and jeans that she entered the club wearing. When she reached down and laced up her all black Jordans, Envy spoke up.

"Where are you going? You're up after Selena."

"I'm going home. If Rico asks where I'm at, tell him I got sick."

"You tell him yourself. I'm not getting yelled at because of you."

"Fine." Asanti returned the lock to her locker and threw her purse strap over her shoulder. "I'll tell him myself." She strutted out the room with Envy's eyes following behind.

She's About That Life: Familiar Territory – Keisha Elle

Asanti was a few feet away from Rico's closed door when she heard his muffled voice. He was talking to someone. Asanti tiptoed closer.

"Five girls? That's gonna stop a lot of traffic in my spot. How much are you talking?"

Silence.

"Come on now. One of my girls can make that in a night. I've been in the game a long time and we've done business before. Don't try that bullshit with me."

More Silence.

"Now you're talking my language. Swing by the office tomorrow and we'll iron out the details."

Asanti heard silence and then movement within the office. She tried to speed off without getting caught, but her feet just weren't fast enough. Rico opened the door,

She's About That Life: Familiar Territory – Keisha Elle

stepping out to see Asanti speed walking in the opposite direction.

"Aye, yo Duchess!"

Damn, she thought to herself. She should have gone with her gut instinct and left without telling Rico anything. If she had, she would have been out of there already.

"Yes."

"Can I talk to you for a minute?"

She let out a loud sigh. Asanti turned around and walked back towards Rico.

"What's wrong?" he asked, not sure how to read Asanti's expression.

"It's always bad when you're called to the principal's office, right?" Asanti walked past Rico into his office.

She's About That Life: Familiar Territory – Keisha Elle

"Not for me. I wanted to fuck the shit out of my principal." He grinned closing the door behind him.

"What do you want Rico? I was on my way home?"

"You're leaving? There's money to be made."

"The other girls need it more than me. Especially Diana. She's about to have another mouth to feed and she can't dance forever. I've already worked five days this week."

"That bitch doesn't bring in half as much money as you do. I can't let you go tonight."

"I'm leaving." Asanti walked towards the door. She heard Rico's cell phone ring behind her.

"Jay, my man."

Asanti stopped in her tracks. She turned on her heels. Jace was on the phone and Rico had the power to

She's About That Life: Familiar Territory – Keisha Elle

spill everything. Since the party, their relationship was cordial. She knew that he wanted more, and a part of her did too. She didn't know how he would react if he found out that she worked at Club Fantasy.

"Asanti? She's a bad one. How'd you luck up on that?" He grinned in Asanti's direction. "Yeah, I know what you mean." He licked his lips. "You know what?" Rico looked as if a bright idea fell out the sky and hit him right at that moment. "As a matter of fact I do. I see her all the time."

Asanti frantically shook her head. Rico was about to tell Jace everything and she could not let that happen.

"I'll stay," she whispered.

Rico smiled. He had Asanti right where he wanted her.

She's About That Life: Familiar Territory – Keisha Elle

"Yeah man, she's friends with my girl. I'll see if I can find that information out for you. Aye, are you on this side of town? I got some girls I'm sure you'd love to see."

He was fucking with Asanti now and she didn't like it one bit. She could feel her temperature rising.

"I got this new redbone." Rico stared directly at Asanti as he spoke. "Her head game is worth every penny. Come on down. It'll be on the house."

Asanti thought she was going to be sick. This was not happening. She stood there watching Rico get his rocks off. He was manipulating the situation, and loving every minute doing it.

"Well, maybe next time. Aight bro."

Rico hung up the phone. He looked at his watch before barking orders in Asanti's direction.

She's About That Life: Familiar Territory – Keisha Elle

"You're up in fifteen minutes. I want you dressed and ready to go."

"You're an asshole, do you know that?"

"You don't get far in my profession being nice, sweetheart. Now, you have fourteen minutes."

Asanti sighed loudly before grabbing the door handle.

"Oh, and Duchess, I wouldn't tell Komiko about club business if I were you. I don't want to have to tell both Komiko and Jace about how deep your throat is. I know from experience, remember."

"You wouldn't."

"Try me. You have thirteen minutes."

She's About That Life: Familiar Territory – Keisha Elle

Asanti flung the door open without responding. She wanted to get the hell away from Rico as fast as she could. He wasn't done playing with her yet.

"One last thing. One of my client's asked for five girls for next Saturday. A private gig. It's paying real nice. Clear your calendar."

"I don't do parties Rico."

"You do now."

She's About That Life: Familiar
Territory – Keisha Elle

She's About That Life: Familiar Territory – Keisha Elle

Chapter 9

Asanti applied a thin layer of lip gloss to her pouty lips. She batted her eyes a few times, making sure her mascara was not clumpy and her lashes were curled to perfection. Usually when she saw one of her family members, she would entertain them with a make-up free face and a decent pair of jeans. Today, she added a little more effort. A black wrap dress hugged her tight frame. Her usually curly brown ringlets were bone straight, hanging towards the center of her back.

A loud knock at the door startled her. She took a deep breath before letting her black heeled sandals stomp the six steps towards the door. Quickly turning around to give the living room one last once over, she turned the handle and opened the door.

She's About That Life: Familiar Territory – Keisha Elle

Kat waddled in first. Her swollen feet were stuffed in a pair of ballet flats. The overinflated basketball in the front of her body hung low as she slowly walked.

"Hey Kat." Asanti embraced her immediately. "Is that baby ever going to come."

"That's what I want to know. My due date was two days ago, and he hasn't even budged." She continued waddling her way through the apartment in frustration.

"Hey sis," Shawn said, walking in and hugging his sister tightly. He was glad that she reached out and called them all over. Things had been strained between the family, and it was time for everyone to put their feelings aside and let everything out in the open. "Something sure smells good! Man, I'm hungry."

She's About That Life: Familiar Territory – Keisha Elle

Asanti gave Shawn a playful push. He always had a positive vibe about him. He was just an all-around likeable guy.

David walked in next. He missed his daughter, but he didn't want to force a relationship on her. He knew that she still harbored ill feelings from the past. He extended his arms for a hug. Asanti stepped into her father's embrace. When he tightened around her like a boa constrictor, she could feel the positive transfer of energy.

"Thanks for inviting me." David kissed his daughter on the cheek before proceeding inside.

Cynthia and Sidney stayed on David's heels. Besides a quick nod in Asanti's direction, they didn't even speak.

"This is a nice place," David said taking a seat in the newly purchased leather recliner. Komiko gave Asanti full reign over decorating ideas. In the two months since

She's About That Life: Familiar Territory – Keisha Elle

arriving in Atlanta, the entire apartment had undergone a drastic makeover.

"Thanks dad." Asanti blushed, happy to have her father's approval.

"I've never been on this side of town. How is it?" Now he was pressing for information.

"It's quiet. I like it."

"It must run you a pretty penny every month. What did you say your roommate did again?"

"She's a model. She into acting too. She wanted to formally meet everyone, but a job came up that she just couldn't turn down. She left yesterday."

"Sounds like she's gone a lot, baby girl. I don't know how I feel about you being home by yourself."

"Jace lives right across the hall," Shawn interjected. "It must be a cool spot if my boy lives here. She's fine."

She's About That Life: Familiar Territory – Keisha Elle

"You know I worry." David rubbed his forehead and fixed his eyes on a large colorful painting of an African woman balancing a large bowl on her head.

"Dad, I'm fine, really." Asanti watched Kat shift in her seat uncomfortably. She sat with her legs open – definitely a no-no for a grown woman. Her long dress covered her opened legs.

"What are you doing for money?"

The question hit Asanti like a Mack truck. She knew one day this conversation would come up. Right now was not the time. Both her father and brother were respected lawyers in Atlanta. Even Sidney had recently started law school at Emory University. Everyone had something positive going for themselves, except Asanti. Amongst all of their success, her degree in Economics felt more like a disappointment.

She's About That Life: Familiar Territory – Keisha Elle

"I have a job. It's not at a law firm like you or Shawn, but it's a job. It pays the bills." Omitting the truth was not the same as lying.

"It's a family business baby girl. You are just as much a part of this family as everyone else. I worked hard to ensure that."

"Where's your bathroom?" Sidney stood up quickly. In typical Sidney fashion, she ended the conversation. If it didn't benefit her, she wanted no part of it.

"It's around the corner, I'll show you."

Asanti led the way to a half bathroom, close to the living room area. She made sure that she cleaned the bathroom thoroughly before her family arrived. She was expecting Cynthia and Sidney to make an excuse as to why they wouldn't be attending the dinner that she planned. In the event that they came, which they did, she didn't want to

She's About That Life: Familiar Territory – Keisha Elle

give the uppity bitches anything to talk about. Sidney

entered the open bathroom door and quickly shut it. Asanti

returned to her waiting family.

"Well, I guess we can get started." She led her

family into the small kitchen. The space was not ideal, but

everyone had a place to sit comfortable. Six suede chairs

lined the large glass table.

Everyone took a seat. The table was already set with

thick porcelain plates atop black place mats. Asanti pulled a

large pan of the lasagna out of the oven. Using oven mits,

she placed the pan on a serving tray in the middle of the

table.

Sidney retreated from the bathroom and took a seat

next to Shawn. Asanti would be forced to sit in between the

two people in the room she despised most - Sidney and

Cynthia.

She's About That Life: Familiar Territory – Keisha Elle

Like a good host, Asanti served all of her guests. After placing a portion of lasagna on their plates, she added a slice of garlic bread and a small side salad. Everyone sat in quiet anticipation. When she finally took her seat, she bowed her head and started a prayer.

"Lord, thank you for this food we are about to receive for the nourishment of our bodies. Please allow the food to give us strength and an open mind as we discuss topics that may be uncomfortable for us. I know some of the people at my table don't like me, and I'm okay with that. Just let us all act like adults and everything will be okay. In your name I pray Lord. Amen."

Several low Amens followed before Asanti spoke again.

"I'll start." She poured Italian dressing on her salad.

She's About That Life: Familiar Territory – Keisha Elle

"Dad, you haven't always been as supportive as I would have liked you to be." She refused to make eye contact. "I feel like you don't want me around."

"That's not true."

Asanti took a small bite of her salad. It needed more dressing. She looked up after the second bite.

"That's how you make me feel."

"I'm sorry you feel that way. That was never my intention. I didn't want you to leave. You made that choice and I respected it. I've always been here for you, just like I always will be."

An uncomfortable silence filled the room. This was not the type of conversation everyone expected to have. Pain was evident in both of their voices. Years of raw pain.

"But dad, I was kid. I was made to feel like I was an intruder in your home. You had another family and I didn't fit into that equation. I felt like you didn't want me there. No one wanted me there."

"It wasn't like that sis," Shawn began, reaching for a napkin to wipe his mouth. "We were all young. Sid and I had issues too. We had to leave our father, and then David came along. I didn't want to like him. I didn't want my mom to marry him. Blended families can be difficult. Kids go through that shit with stepparents." He turned to his mother, "Excuse my language, but it's true. David is a great man, and I've learned a lot from him. Life is too short to harbor ill feelings baby sis." A large forkful of lasagna entered his mouth, momentarily silencing him. Asanti used that as her cue to continue.

"That's not how I saw it."

Asanti took a bite of her lasagna. As usual, it was perfect. That's one of the only things her mother taught her. Julissa could make a meal out of almost anything. She

She's About That Life: Familiar Territory – Keisha Elle

dreamed of going to school and becoming a chef, but men with long money interested her more. Asanti was barely out the womb when Julissa left, leaving the responsibility of raising her daughter to her parents.

"Why is everyone acting like this is okay?" Sidney was tired of the blame game taking place in front of her. She was ready to go. As good as the food looked, she wouldn't have been surprised if Asanti poisoned it. "She is not a baby. You have to have tough skin in this world. All that sad shit is for the birds."

"You always have something to say." Asanti cut her eyes at Sidney. Who the hell did she think she was?

"You're damn right! You have this sense of entitlement and its getting on my nerves."

"Chill out Sid." Shawn tried his best to deescalate the situation. He knew that both his sisters were hard-headed and feisty. It was easier said than done. All the

She's About That Life: Familiar Territory – Keisha Elle

yelling was not good for his pregnant fiancée. He placed

his hand on Sidney's arm in an attempt to calm her down.

"I will not! Why is everyone acting like she's not

the problem. She is! She walks in my mother's house and

does whatever she wants."

"Your mother's house?" Asanti thought she heard

incorrectly.

"Yes, my mother's house. When David asked my

mother to marry him, what was his, became hers."

"What the hell is your problem Sidney? I don't

know why you and your mother don't like me. I have never

done anything to either one of you."

"I've never said I didn't like you." Cynthia began in

a low motherly tone. She was obviously putting on a show

for David. "You have a way of always playing the victim.

You have tried several times to interfere with my marriage

with your father. And yes, I told him that I didn't trust you and that I would prefer for you to not come over. That's because of your actions. You have hurt this man time and time again." She pointed to David who was sitting back in his chair wearing a dumb, tired look on his face. "Whenever you don't get your way, you leave. You never face your problems, you just run."

"Why are you even here? Did you fuck things up in Louisville so bad that now you have to run back to Atlanta? You're like the plague and I'd rather you stay as far away from me as possible. I don't need this shit." Sidney stood up so hard that her chair fell back. It made a loud thud noise when it hit the ground.

"Don't leave sis." Shawn tried pleading with his sister.

"I'm out. I can't do this anymore." She looked in Asanti's direction and shook her head. "I don't know what kind of game you're playing, but count me out of it. You're

She's About That Life: Familiar Territory – Keisha Elle

a sad excuse for a woman, always has been, always will be."

"Watch your mouth Sidney. That's enough." David hated to see the women he loved argue and fight. "I really wish that you two could get along. I just don't understand it. Where is this all coming from?"

The sound that escaped Kat's lips silenced the room. She immediately grabbed her stomach as cramps worse than menstrual pains tore through her insides.

"What's wrong?" Shawn turned to his girlfriend.

"I think I just had a contraction." The tightening of her uterus was slowly relaxing.

"It's probably those Braxton things." Cynthia snapped her finger repeated, trying to think of the correct name.

She's About That Life: Familiar Territory – Keisha Elle

"Braxton-Hicks." Kat's voice was back to normal. "I've been having those for a couple of months but that one just…"

Kat didn't even finish her sentence before a sound similar to a wounded dog was released. She cried out in gut-wrenching pain.

"I'm taking you to the hospital." Shawn stood up, grabbing Kat's arm with him.

"We're coming with you." Cynthia said, glad for the excuse to leave.

The door slammed shut as Asanti remained seated. Everyone had quickly exited the condo without a second thought. Once again, they were all one big happy family, and she was just an outsider.

She used her fork to play around in her lasagna. After the tense interaction, she no longer had an appetite.

She's About That Life: Familiar Territory – Keisha Elle

She's About That Life: Familiar Territory – Keisha Elle

She's About That Life: Familiar Territory – Keisha Elle

Chapter 10

Asanti surfed the internet for ideas. The private party that she was being forced to dance at was only a couple of days away. Although she had numerous kinky outfits to choose from, she wanted something different, something to make herself stand out. Rico might have been sending five girls, but she was determined to walk out of there with the most money. After the disastrous dinner with her family, she threw herself into her work. She had a new goal – plan for the future. Besides Komiko and Rico, no one knew that she took her clothes off for a living. She was embarrassed to tell anyone this aspect of her life. She was obviously in the wrong profession.

As usual, Komiko was gone. She was home for less than twenty-four hours before she was called out for another project. Komiko was glad to be consistently working. She had friends waiting around for their next gig,

She's About That Life: Familiar Territory – Keisha Elle

and she was booked solid for the whole month. If she played her cards right, she would be working the next month too. Asanti was truly happy for her friend's success, but coming home to an empty condo daily was getting old fast.

The sound of laughter coming from the hallway momentarily distracted her. She was browsing shear thongs when the laughter increased. The differences in pitch told her that it was a man and a woman. Expecting the laughs to stop once they passed her door, she continued scanning the pages of the online catalog. The hyena-like laughing stopped outside her door and increased in intensity.

Asanti retreated from the couch, walking on the plush carpet with her ankle socks. She peeked out of the peephole trying to get a look at the perpetrators. When she didn't see anyone, she strutted back in the direction of her comfy chair. The laughter returned. This time, the

She's About That Life: Familiar Territory – Keisha Elle

accompanying sound of something hitting the wall frustrated her. Someone was going to learn that day. She walked over and snatched the door open, not knowing what to expect. Her irritation gave her the courage to confront the nuisance. When she saw Jace and Raven laughing like there was no tomorrow, she turned her nose up in disgust.

"There are other people in this building you know." Her voice was cold, watching the way Raven's hands just happened to lightly grab Jace's forearm. He acted like he didn't notice.

The pair stopped laughing, finally noticing Asanti standing just outside her doorway. They tried to gain their composure, but a couple of small laughs seemed to escape Raven's thin lips. At that moment, Asanti realized where she remembered Raven from. She had seen her entering Jace's apartment with him. She was the one he would leave with at night and come back wearing gym clothes. Judging by their attire now, that's exactly where they had been.

"Um, I'll see you tomorrow Jace." Raven gave him a 'call me and let me know how it goes' look before turning on her heels and walking away. She didn't even look in Asanti's direction. Asanti watched as her flat ass barely moved in her tight yoga pants.

She walked back into her apartment and attempted to close the door. Jace called out to her.

"Can we talk?"

"What do you want Jace? It's late and I have to..."

"I just want to talk. Can I come in?"

Reluctantly, Asanti stepped aside, allowing Jace to enter with his large bag in tow. He was taken aback by the new décor. He took one look at the walls filled with African art, and instantly knew it was Asanti's doing. Jace

She's About That Life: Familiar Territory – Keisha Elle

took a seat on the oversized sofa and tossed his bag to the side. He sat back, enjoying the feel of the comfy pillows.

Asanti stood close, her arms crossed in front of her chest. She wished she had put on a robe or even changed clothes completely. The crop top and boy shorts that she wore barely covered anything. It was comfortable and in the privacy of her own home, she usually wore far less. She wasn't thinking when she let her irritation get the best of her. If she were, she would not have walked out and confronted Raven and Jace for making too much noise. Jace wouldn't be sitting on her couch at that moment, staring at her with hungry eyes.

"What do you want?"

"Shawn asked me to check on you. He was expecting you at the hospital. Kat had her baby."

"I heard. I figured she already had enough people up there." She visibly relaxed and took a seat directly across from Jace. "I got the pics he sent. I just haven't had a chance to respond yet."

"Why not?"

Asanti changed the subject.

"It's kinda late for you to be out on a week day isn't it?" The hour hand on the clock pointed to Roman numeral XI, while the minute hand pointed vertically on Roman numeral VI.

Jace smiled, showing off his pearly whites.

"Why do you care what time I get home? Were you waiting up?"

"Don't flatter yourself. For your information, I was on my computer. I wouldn't have even known you were home if you two weren't making so much noise." Asanti eyed the computer sitting comfortably next to Jace. It didn't cross her mind to grab it when she sat down. She stood, reaching for the computer, still opened to a pair of red see-

She's About That Life: Familiar Territory – Keisha Elle

through thongs lined with lace. Jace's hands were quicker than hers. With the swipe of his finger across the mouse pad, the page opened up to a model's backside in the thin material.

Asanti's face flushed crimson. Even though there was nothing wrong with wearing a thong, the fact that Jace knew she was looking at one embarrassed the shit out of her. She felt like some sort of freak instead of a woman old enough to do what she damn well pleased.

"You would look good in that."

"How do you know?" It was hard to keep up her tough girl act when she began to feel her nipples slowly harden at his compliment.

"You look good in anything you put on. Even now."

Her nipples were standing at full attention. She was all giddy inside. It had been a long time since she felt like a woman. A real woman. Rico had made her body feel good, but it wasn't the same. Jace could evoke emotions that no other man could ever reach. Even Justin couldn't compete. Jace was the total package.

"So what's up with you and Raven?" Asanti crossed her arms over her hardened nipples and changed the subject. It was obvious that Raven had a thing for him, but she couldn't read if the feeling was mutual. She watched the smile form on Jace's face.

"Are you jealous?"

Was he serious? Of course she was jealous, but she would never let him know that. He could have attempted to hide the big ass grin on his face, but like a man, he didn't.

"Why would I be? You're not my man."

Jace fixed his lips to say something, but relaxed them instead. Asanti expected a harsh comeback or something slick enough to shut her up for good. He surprised her when he stood up and walked over to join her

She's About That Life: Familiar Territory – Keisha Elle

on the oversized round swivel chair. She froze, her heartbeat beating in rapid succession. He was inches away from her. His body smelled like fresh bath soap. Jace smoothed a strand of hair out of her face and placed it behind her ear. He wanted to look deep into her large, hazel eyes.

"Raven is a friend. We dated in the past, it didn't work out. That's it. We work together now. Sometimes we go to the gym together. She's just as dedicated to staying in shape as I am."

"You don't smell like you just came from the gym." She couldn't think of anything else to say. It was true though.

"I shower at the gym before leaving. That's why I take a bag." He pointed to the gym bag sitting across from them. "You've asked a lot of questions about me. What about you?"

She's About That Life: Familiar Territory – Keisha Elle

"What do you mean?"

"I haven't seen any men coming in and out of the apartment, so I'm guessing that you're single, right?"

"Are you apartment stalking?"

It was Jace's turn to seem offended.

"Me? No, I was just trying to get a glimpse of the beautiful woman across the hall. You know you haven't changed much, ya know."

Asanti blushed. Jace always did have a way with words.

"You don't have to say things like that to me." Asanti attempted to stand, but Jace grabbed her arm, pulling her back down. He was tired of her always running away. "No stay. Please."

He ran his hands down her soft face. His thumbs traced the lining of her lips. Leaning in, and taking a chance, he kissed them softly. When Asanti didn't resist, he

She's About That Life: Familiar Territory – Keisha Elle

leaned in again and planted another soft kiss. Using his tongue to part her lips, he graciously entered when she slowly opened. Their tongues danced a gentle dance, wrapping around each other like a slow rumba. Asanti broke the kiss.

"I'm sorry. I've just been wanting to do that for so long."

"It's not you. Really. It's just…Can I ask you a question?"

"Of course." He wasn't sure what it had to do with anything, but he wanted her, and would answer any question that she asked.

"When I used to live with my dad, I saw a picture of you with your arm around a girl. It was at Kat's birthday party. It was a long time ago. I don't know if you remember or not, but you looked really happy and…" Her voice

She's About That Life: Familiar Territory – Keisha Elle

drifted off trying to find the right words. "Why didn't you tell me you had a girlfriend?"

Jace's forehead wrinkled in confusion. He thought back on the day Asanti called him, cursing him out. It was so random and unexpected, that he didn't know how to react. He had made last minute stop to meet Shawn before going home and studying for exams. It was Kat's birthday, and he wanted to at least show his face. When he got there, Sidney insisted on a group photo. Her best friend stood to the side watching everyone's smiling face.

"Come on Noelle," Jace said, motioning her to join in the picture.

Displaying a shy smile, she held her hands up and shook her head.

"No, I'm fine."

She's About That Life: Familiar Territory – Keisha Elle

"Come on." He wrapped his arm around her shoulders and pulled her in close. "You know you're one of us." The photo was taking and everyone smiled brightly.

Jace never understood what he did wrong. He tried numerous times to call her after she left. He left message after message. All his calls went unreturned. His heart was conflicted. He yearned for the young girl who had completely turned him out. He wanted to be with her, but his conscience told him that it was best to just stay away. She was young, and his best friend's sister. David McCoy trusted him. He had already betrayed his trust by messing with Asanti in the first place. Regardless of how genuine his feelings were, it wasn't right, and his conscience told him so. After a while, he let the situation go. If it was meant to be, fate would allow Asanti to re-enter his life. To him, it was one hell of a coincidence that she now lived right across the hall.

She's About That Life: Familiar Territory – Keisha Elle

"I didn't have a girlfriend."

"Sidney showed me a picture of you at Kat's birthday party with your arm…" Asanti stopped mid-sentence. Her eyes brightened as if an exciting new idea popped into her head.

"Sidney? Really? As much as you two go back and forth, you believed something Sidney said."

"I just saw the picture. Your arms were around her."

"Shhh." Jace placed his finger against her full lips. "The only person I wanted my arms around was you. I was feeling you. Bad as hell. I just didn't think it was fair to keep you a secret, so I stopped trying to call when you left. I respect David and Shawn is my boy. I didn't know what exactly I did, but I figured the separation was for the best." He placed another light kiss on her lips. "I don't want to dwell on the past. Let's focus on the present."

She's About That Life: Familiar Territory – Keisha Elle

Asanti visibly relaxed. The ill-feelings that she harbored for so long, slowly left her mind. She didn't understand why she hadn't put two and two together a long time ago. She could have saved herself many sleepless nights.

Her thoughts drifted to better places when Jace began trailing small kisses from her lips, down to her collarbone. Her nipples hardened into miniature pebbles when he bent down and kissed them through her shirt. She moaned softly, allowing him to have his way with her. He stood up grabbing Asanti's hand in his. She stood beside him. He turned her around, dropped to his knees and slowly slid her shorts down from behind. She wore no panties. Her thighs were already wet with her juices. He pushed her forward, back onto the chair. She was ass up, mounted on all fours. Jace licked his lips, ready to taste the sweet candy that he'd craved for over three years.

She's About That Life: Familiar Territory – Keisha Elle

He went in face first, spreading her cheeks wide while he flicked at her clit with his tongue. When he stiffened his tongue and entered her juicy hole, she couldn't remain still. She bucked back and forth, fucking his face in the process. Stopping momentarily to enter her with his a thick finger, he returned his mouth to her clit.

"Jace, I'm about to cum!" Asanti yelled breathlessly, feeling the familiar jolt of energy slowly increasing in intensity. He sucked hard, taking her over the top. He lapped up her sweet juices as her body convulsed.

"Turn over."

She did as she was told. Asanti hadn't fully recovered from her first orgasm when Jace started the intense assault on her clit once again. Her inner muscles tensed, her body shook repeated, and Jace's name slipped off her tongue.

She's About That Life: Familiar Territory – Keisha Elle

Asanti didn't even have time to gain her composure before Jace inserted himself, deep inside her. It felt like his ten inches was more like a foot long. Her pussy muscles wrapped around him like a glove, holding on for dear life with every stroke.

"Damn girl," was all he could mutter as he leaned forward, grabbing a firm hold of her breasts. It had been a while since she had been fucked so good. He filled her to the brim and she was taking it like a champ.

They were both in their own passionate world when the front door closing startled them. They both looked up in embarassment to see Komiko shaking her head. Jace stopped mid-stroke, his dick instantly softened and slid out of Asanti's super wet pussy.

Komiko walked past them as if she saw people fucking in her apartment on a daily basis. She stopped just out of eyesight of the living room.

She's About That Life: Familiar Territory – Keisha Elle

"I want my chair professionally cleaned when you're done." With that, she entered her bedroom and closed the door. Her television could be heard powering on, the volume slowly increased until it was loud as hell.

Blood rushed back to Jace's manhood. Within seconds, he was hard again and ready to finish what he started.

"Put it in," Asanti said breathy, feeling his pole graze her leg. She inhaled deeply, as he followed directions and inserted himself once again.

She's About That Life: Familiar Territory – Keisha Elle

She's About That Life: Familiar Territory – Keisha Elle

Chapter 11

The windows were fogged with a thick cloud of smoke. Two blunts were in rotation. Asanti waived off the second blunt, still feeling comfortable from the first. Her eyes followed the plastic bag filled with white powder being passed in Envy's direction. That was something she wouldn't be passing up.

"Oh, so you want this hunh?" Envy dangled the partially empty bag in front of Asanti's face. She was not in the damn mood.

Asanti snatched it from Envy's fingers, careful not to tear the bag and release its contents.

"Do you know who the party is for?" Selena asked squeezing her nose, trying to ease the burning sensation going up her nostrils. She swallowed hard, remnants of the wasted drug oozing down her throat.

She's About That Life: Familiar Territory – Keisha Elle

"Rico didn't tell me." Envy used her fingernail to snort a quick hit.

"Diana, you're fucking his ass. Did he say anything to you?" Envy questioned.

"He didn't say anything to me." Diana sat quietly in the back of the SUV. Dressed in a simple black bra and thong set, patent leather stilettos and a long trench coat, tied at the waist, she was ready to get the night over with. It wouldn't be long before her dinner decided to make an entrance.

"It's for some bachelor party, bachelorette party, something like that. I don't know what you call it." The new girl with the massive Size G breasts and even bigger ass said. She was feeling relaxed from the good weed being passed around. She waved off the coke. White lines had never been her thing. She saw too many cokeheads willing to sell their souls for the white stuff.

She's About That Life: Familiar Territory – Keisha Elle

"A bachelorette party? We're dancing for some bitches?" Envy's interest peaked. This was right up her alley.

"No, No, No. It's one of those new things crazy people are doing. They're having a Bachelor party and a Bachelorette party all in one. They hired us to entertain the men and I think they have male dancers for the women."

"That's the craziest shit I ever heard." Envy slipped her arms into her trench coat. Wrapping it around her naked body, she tied it loosely at the waist.

Asanti lay silent, barely moving. The up and down movements of her chest confirmed she was still breathing. A lightweight in the drug game, she was high. Higher than high. High as hell actually. She hadn't felt that good in a long time. Nothing was going to push her off cloud nine except Father Time himself.

She's About That Life: Familiar Territory – Keisha Elle

"Come on girls," Envy shook Asanti roughly causing her to sit up. Her hair was disheveled and her bra twisted, exposing her firm titties. Envy licked her lips in excitement. "Big Zeke is out there. That means they're ready for us."

Asanti, Envy, Diana, Selena, and the new girl, nicknamed New New by the other dancers, hopped out the SUV, one by one. Envy overloaded their bodies with fruity body spray. It covered the familiar scent of good weed and tickled your nose at the same time. It would have to work. They each wore tan trench coats, hiding their goodies underneath, with small bags containing personal items. Each girl had a face beat for the gods, long ponytail, stiletto boots.

Envy led the way, her confidence at an all-time high. This was not her first rodeo. In fact, she enjoyed dancing at parties. She pulled in big money at events like this and today was not going to be an exception. Her thigh high stilettos stomped confidently toward the former marine with a buzz cut and the word security written across his snug shirt.

"There you are ladies. I was just about to put in a call."

"Well now you don't have to." Envy shot back, understanding what he meant. He was preparing to call and tell Rico the girls were a no show. He was her least favorite doorman, bouncer, whatever you wanted to call him, at Club Fantasy. He wasn't worth a damn. If something popped off, she'd better be able to fend for herself, because Big Zeke was a muscular ball of pure softness.

Big Zeke led the way through the main lobby area, and down the hall to a large room. The words MAIN CONFERENCE ROOM were embroidered on a steel wall sign. A large makeshift sign stuck to one of the doors. A

She's About That Life: Familiar Territory – Keisha Elle

man and a woman, posed together kissing with fireworks going off overhead. Their names boldly sat atop their picture: Liz and Cedric.

"Where are we supposed to freshen up at Zeke?" Envy looked around, seeing nothing but a long hallway and closed doors.

"Right here."

"You must be kidding me. We always get a room to ourselves."

"Not this time Sweetheart." Big Zeke smirked. "Rico said there's enough room right out here." He spun around, his hand extended, showing the girls a hallway full of nothing.

"This isn't right Zeke and you know it!" Envy was heated. One thing she knew Big Zeke didn't do, was lie. Rico obviously didn't give a damn. He hadn't reserved a separate room for them, like he usually did.

She's About That Life: Familiar Territory – Keisha Elle

"That's how it goes. You ladies have five minutes."

Zeke walked off, joining a newly arrived bouncer. Asanti

remembered him from the first time she entered Club

Paradise. She instantly remembered his northern accent.

When she learned that he went by the name New York, she

wasn't surprised.

Five minutes wasn't a lot of time. They all worked

together, adjusting weaves, freshening up make-up, and

calming nerves. Asanti stood flawless in a one-piece see

through body suit. She originally planned on wearing a bra

and thong set underneath, but quickly decided against it.

There would be no teasing today. She was getting straight

to the point.

Envy decided to go commando. Her dark, flawless

frame was made to be seen. Her nipples were already hard

and ready to make money.

She's About That Life: Familiar Territory – Keisha Elle

New New helped Diana tie her sheer halter top. Her high waist boy shorts were unflattering to her growing figure, but she wore it anyway. New New wore a bright pink thong and bra set. She outshined Diana with her looks alone. Her toffee skin was freshly tanned. Standing next to her, Diana looked like an amateur.

Selena stood off to the side, talking low in to her cell phone. Everyone knew that Selena always called her two daughters every night at exactly 8:45PM. She finished her call and handed her phone to Big Zeke for safe keepings. The girls lined up and watched as Big Zeke grabbed one of the handles of the French doors and slowly opened it.

The large room was dim. Seats were scattered around, leaving a small area, right in the middle of the room. They easily maneuvered through the seated guests. Asanti followed closely behind Envy, swatting at roaming hands in the process. Selena, Diana, and New New followed behind her, enduring the same treatment.

A mixture of cheap colognes and perfumes filled the air. Asanti held her breath, hoping her allergies would remain under control. She sped up her pace, almost walking on Envy's heels. She was glad when she reached the makeshift stage area and passed the overwhelming aroma.

The music began without warning. Asanti stood frozen, nervous in the foreign environment. Envy immediately went in, backing her ass up towards the closest seat she could find. The strong hands wrapping around her and pulling her towards an awaiting lap were undoubtedly male. She grinded her ass in his crotch. Lifting her large breasts with his hands, he stuffed several bills under each one.

New New found her way to the back of the room. The lighting was not as dim back there. An older gentleman leaning against a wall was in need of some one-on-one attention. She grabbed his crotch through his pants. It stiffened immediately. Placing her ass firmly against his erection, she pushed back and rolled her hips. He grabbed her breasts tightly, enjoying the sexual contact.

Selena and Diana followed each other closely. They didn't attempt to compete for attention like Envy. She was there to work, and so were they. The two bestfriends used a different approach. They began working the crowd, giving lap dances to anyone extending money in their direction.

"Come on girl. Let's see what you're working with." A deep voice rang out, snapping Asanti out of her daze.

Everyone was occupied and getting money, except her. She was still higher than a kite, but if she didn't get to moving, money was going to pass her by. There was no way she was letting any of the other girls take food from

She's About That Life: Familiar Territory – Keisha Elle

her plate. She eased herself in front of him. Tuning everyone else out, she gave him her undivided attention. It was as if he was the only one in the room. His masculine face was sexy as hell and the bulge in the front of his pants leaning comfortable to the left told her what time it was. He was ready to spend some money. *Let's get it*, she thought to herself.

"Of course baby."

Asanti straddled him, lowering the top of her bodysuit down to free her firm breasts. They were visible all along, but something about seeing them free of material turned men on. The cutie attempting to put one of her hardened nipples in his mouth was no different. Asanti leaned back, teasing him in the process.

"Only a hoe works for free baby."

She's About That Life: Familiar Territory – Keisha Elle

"Is that right?" Mr. Cute face licked his lips and smiled. "Do you offer a 'This is my last night as a free man' special?"

"Freebies don't pay the bills." She leaned closer, allowing him to put of her nipples into his mouth. When he loosened his grip, she leaned back again, stopping him from another attempt "But I promise it'll be worth it."

"I'm sure you will. What's your name?" He slid closer to the edge of his chair, balancing Asanti expertly on his lap. He reached into the pocket of his jeans, while waiting on Asanti's reply.

"It doesn't matter."

He pulled some money from his pocket and held it in Asanti's direction without even counting it.

"I want to know."

"Duchess."

She's About That Life: Familiar Territory – Keisha Elle

"Well Duchess, if you're anything like that girl over there," he pointed in New New's direction, "Let me know. We can go upstairs to my room."

New New was against the wall, fucking - hard. Her loud moans and exaggerated screams overshadowed the music. Ironically, no one seemed care. There was no way in hell that they didn't notice. New New was butt naked, enjoying the older man's average, but thick dick. Fully dressed, with only his manhood exposed, he pumped in and out quickly. He had stamina for a man who appeared to be in his late forties. His graying hair made it clear that he wasn't a young buck, but the way he was handling New New's barely legal ass, he put men half his age to shame.

Selena and Diana continued to walk around, giving quick lap dances and shaking their titties for a couple of dollars. They both had pretty faces, but lacked the got-getter attitude of a top dancer. When the money started

She's About That Life: Familiar Territory – Keisha Elle

drying up, Diana exited the room, hoping that Big Zeke wouldn't run his mouth to Rico. She was tired. Her pregnant hormones were telling her to sit her ass down.

Selena continued to dance, trying hard to make her money. Her two daughters were her world. Every dollar that she made was spent on them, and she loved putting a smile on their face. When a strong hand cupped one of her ass cheeks and squeezed hard, she didn't resist. He came out his pocket, handing her a wad of bills. She looked through the thick stack, realizing that she wasn't dealing with dollars. This guy wanted something, and it wasn't just a dance. Two thick fingers inched towards her middle. When they pulled her thong to the side and slipped into her wet opening, she didn't resist. You had to pay to play, and this man was paid in full.

Envy danced alone, attracting her own crowd of eager men wishing they could get just a piece of her dark

She's About That Life: Familiar Territory – Keisha Elle

chocolate. Her body moved with the rhythm of the beat, swaying, bucking, and popping in all directions. She let a couple men grab on her titties and ass a couple times, but until there were more bills in front of her with Jackson, Grant, or better yet Franklin on the front, they weren't gonna get close enough to even sniff her pussy.

Asanti threw her head back closing her eyes. She was grinding hard, pretending that it was Jace's lap she was on. It was his hands that she wished were squeezing her ass at that moment. She loved the feel of his strong body underneath her.

She was so caught up in the moment that she didn't notice the light slowly taking over the room. Mr. 'I'm getting married tomorrow' released his grip and damn near pushed Asanti to the floor. Her eyes shot open, catching a glimpse of the gang of angry women ready for war.

She's About That Life: Familiar Territory – Keisha Elle

"What the fuck is this Cedric?" A short, slim woman with long braids twisted into a bun asked. Her pink and white bride-to-be sash told the entire room who the hell she was.

The packed room went quiet. That's when Asanti noticed the large divider separating equal halves of a larger room. It was pushed back half way, partially combing both rooms. Looking through to the other side, Asanti saw a room full of women and a few fully clothed male dancers standing stationary, like deer caught in headlights. Those fools were literally having a Bachelor and Bachelorette party in the same room. New New was right.

"Answer me dammit!" The woman walked closer, with her three-person entourage on her heels. "What the fuck were you doing?"

"Liz, baby, I can explain." The lame excuse slipped off his tongue slowly, giving him time to think of a lie.

She's About That Life: Familiar Territory – Keisha Elle

"Duchess was just dancing, that's all. We agreed that we could both have dancers."

"You must think I'm stupid Cedric! I saw that bitch grinding all over you. It was so loud over here that we had to come over and tell you all to keep it down. I didn't know that I was walking into an orgy."

More women crossed the previously divided room after hearing the Liz yelling loudly. Asanti wished Big Zeke or even New York, would earn their pay and come save her from the embarrassment. It was wishful thinking. Liz continued her verbal assault, throwing obvious jabs in Asanti's direction. Asanti thought about responding back, and telling the mediocre bitch off, but as the number of women in the room increased, she knew the backlash wouldn't be anything nice. Gathering up the little bit of dignity she had left, she power walked towards the door. Envy Selena, and New New followed behind quietly.

She's About That Life: Familiar Territory – Keisha Elle

The loud slap across Cedric's face didn't stop Asanti's retreat. Neither did the name-calling behind her. She was getting the hell out of there. She could handle one bitch, maybe even two, but over a dozen angry emerged and stood behind Liz. Asanti was almost out the door when she heard the voice of the last person she expected to see.

"Leaving so soon."

Asanti turned around to see Sidney walking in her direction..

"What are you doing here?" Asanti couldn't think of anything else. Envy and Selena shifted nervously from side-to-side. Their sad attempt at using their hand to shield their exposed bodies was useless.

"The bride-to-be is a close friend." She looked her stepsister up and down, before Asanti covered her breasts with her hands. "The better question would be, what are you doing here? But judging by the way you look right now, I'd say you're working. Does Jace know about your extracurricular activities?"

"Go to hell Sidney!" Asanti was beyond humiliated. She needed to get out of there and fast. "You don't know what you're talking about."

"Oh, yes I do, Duchess. That's what Cedric called you right? When I'm done, everyone else is gonna know too."

She's About That Life: Familiar Territory – Keisha Elle

Chapter 12

Knock. Knock.

"I'm coming, I'm coming."

Knock. Knock.

"I said I'm fucking coming." Kat yanked the door

open to Asanti's smiling face.

"Hey Kat! Where's my nephew?"

If it was anyone else, Kat would have let them have

it, but because it was Asanti, she bit her tongue for Shawn's

little sister.

"He's in his swing." Kat adjusted the large royal

blue bath towel around her body. She had been in the

shower when Asanti started knocking. After finally getting

her little man to sleep, she was eager to feel the warm water

against her skin.

Asanti's cell phone rung loudly. She looked at the

word PRIVATE pop up on the phone's large screen. She

She's About That Life: Familiar Territory – Keisha Elle

ignored the call, sending it straight to voicemail. The noise caused baby Xavier to cry out loudly. Asanti walked through a small entry way with tiled floors, following the direction of the cry. It wasn't long before she found the newborn, squirming around in his stopped swing.

She freed him from the contraption, watching Kat walk in the opposite direction. His cries became louder when she tried to console him. She didn't know what she was doing wrong. She tried singing to him. That didn't work. She rocked him. That didn't work. He just wasn't having any of it.

"Here." Kat spoke from behind her. When Asanti turned around, Kat was passing a bottle in her direction. "He's hungry."

"How do you know?" Asanti accepted the bottle and placed the soft rubber nipple in his mouth. He latched on immediately and began sucking for dear life.

She's About That Life: Familiar Territory – Keisha Elle

"I know the difference between my son's cries."

Kat excused herself to finish her shower. Asanti used the time to admire her nephew. His gray eyes and fat, chubby body resembled a Cabbage Patch doll. Besides a few strands of hair, he was almost bald. If it wasn't for the brown ear lobes and cuticles, he could have passed for White. Still, Asanti thought he was the cutest baby she had ever seen – even if she was biased.

He finished his bottle and burped loudly after she gave his back a few firm thrusts. When she laid him across her arms to play with his chubby cheeks, his eyes stayed fixed on her face. He was inquisitive and curious. Inadvertently, he stuck his tongue out a few times, never breaking eye contact.

"Hi little man. I'm your Auntie."

The newborn looked confused, not knowing whether to turn away or keep looking at the face in front of

She's About That Life: Familiar Territory – Keisha Elle

him. He made his decision when his mother entered the room. She didn't have to say a word. Kat's presence alone sent him over the edge. His little lips began to quiver and a loud, wailing sound prevailed.

"What did I do?" She looked to Kat for an answer.

"Nothing. He just wants his mommy." Kat grabbed for her son and held him close. Taking a seat beside Asanti on the brown sectional, she slowly rocked her son.

The two chatted like old friends. Two years older than Asanti, she graduated at the top of her class, earning a Master's degree in Finance. She landed her dream job straight out of college, working for a financial consulting firm. When the firm closed down unexpectedly, she began helping around Rainwater & McCoy, LLC as an office assistant. Before long, she was officially hired in as the office manager. It allowed her to spend more time with Shawn, which she loved.

She's About That Life: Familiar Territory – Keisha Elle

Asanti's phone rung again. Once again, the private call was sent to voicemail. Everyone who had her number knew that she did not accept private calls. She was beginning to get irritated. Frustrated, she began twirling the loose ringlets that escaped from her high bun.

"Is everything alright?" Kat rocked her son slowly while turning her attention to Asanti.

"Yeah. Everything's good."

"I worry about you sis…With you all the way on the other side of town and all. You should really consider moving closer to the family."

"Komiko is family."

"You know what I mean." She laid her sleeping son down next to her.

"Kat, I'm not going to kiss anyone's ass. Everyone knows where I stay. No one is breaking their necks to come see how I'm doing."

She's About That Life: Familiar Territory – Keisha Elle

"You're not breaking your neck to see how they're doing either."

"What do you want me to do Kat? Do you want me to call Sidney up like, hey sis, how's it going?" She rolled her eyes at the thought.

"I think you should make an effort."

"I made an effort, and you see how that turned out."

"You two are more alike than you know. You're both stubborn as hell. Can't you see she's jeaous? Her pride won't let her admit that. She was David's baby for years. Then you came along. She feels like she was replaced."

"Replaced? That's bullshit. She spent more time with my dad than I did. We were cool at first. Then she just turned on me. I thought she was just having a bad day or something, but you see how long its lasted."

"Do you think it had something to do with Jace?"

"What? What does Jace have to do with anything?"

She's About That Life: Familiar Territory – Keisha Elle

Kat pushed her long hair off her shoulders.

"You had a thing for Jace. Well, Sidney did too."

Asanti's eyes widened in surprise. She never knew Sidney was interested in Jace.

"He wasn't interested in Sidney, but you were a different story. You know what I mean?"

"No."

"Cut the crap. I know more than you think I know. Jace didn't let just anybody up in his spot."

"We were friends. Nothing more, nothing less."

"Yeah, friends with benefits."

"I don't know what you're talking about."

"Yeah, ok. Well, just so you know, that's where Sidney's problem with you began. She wanted Jace, but he turned her down. Then you come around and everything changed. I guess she didn't understand what you had and she didn't."

She's About That Life: Familiar Territory – Keisha Elle

Asanti finally began to understand the root of Sidney's anger. When Asanti first around in Atlanta at the age of sixteen, they were cool. When Jace started coming over more often, Sidney turned cold. She tried asking Sidney herself, but after receiving the silent treatment, she just gave up. Now things were starting to make sense. It didn't excuse her behavior, but Asanti now knew the cause of Sidney's hatread – jealousy.

"Sidney came to me one day and asked me about you and Jace. At that time, I didn't know anything. I had my own suspicisons though, so I went right to the source and asked Jace."

"What did he say?"

"He said you had some good pussy." Kat smiled at the embarrassed look on Asanti's face. "It's cool, girl. It's just us."

"Do you think Shawn knows?"

She's About That Life: Familiar Territory – Keisha Elle

"I don't think so, but the way Jace sniffs around your ass now, I'm sure it won't be long before he finds out."

"You're silly Kat! We're in a good place right now." Asanti spoke honestly.

"Good as in, you're still fucking him?"

The front door opened, startling Asanti. Her nerves eased when she saw Shawn and Jace walking through the door with two large bags in each hand.

"Hey sis."

"Hi Shawn," Asanti replied, looking in Jace's direction. "Hi Jace."

Jace smiled and nodded towards Asanti. He was trying to play cool, not giving anything away.

"Wait Jace. I'll take those bags." Kat stood up quickly, passing her sleeping son to Asanti. "You can keep Asanti company while I talk to Shawn." Kat gave Asanti a

She's About That Life: Familiar Territory – Keisha Elle

quick wink before grabbing the bags from Jace and disappearing into the kitchen.

Jace took a seat close to Asanti. He sat close enough to smell the vanilla scented perfume that she wore, but not close enough to touch her.

"What's up?" Jace ran his palm over the waves in his hair. It was freshly cut and his facial hair was trimmed just the way Asanti liked it.

"Nothing."

"I haven't seen you in a couple days. Is everything alright?"

"I've been working a lot."

"Do you have anything planned tonight? We can go get a bite to eat."

"Komiko's coming home for a couple of days. I want to be home when she gets here."

She's About That Life: Familiar Territory – Keisha Elle

"We can order something from my place. That way, you'll be home when she arrives."

Asanti contemplated his suggestion. It was early evening, and besides a banana, she hadn't eaten anything all day. It was obvious that he wanted to spend time with her. She wanted to spend time with him too.

Her cell phone went off again, displaying PRIVATE once again. For the fifth time today, she sent the call to voicmail. No messages had been left so far. Whoever was calling wanted to speak to her directly. Jace looked at her, wanting to question her about the call, but knew it wasn't his place. Asanti was glad when Shawn and Kat returned. Shawn walked over and gave his sister a hug.

"I'm glad to see you sis."

Asanti hugged him loosely with one arm. In the other, she still held sleeping Xavier. She ended their embrace and returned to her seat.

She's About That Life: Familiar Territory – Keisha Elle

"So what brings you my way?" Shawn asked, getting straight to the point.

"I came by to see my handsome nephew." She lifted baby Xavier to her pouted lips and kissed him softly on the cheek.

"David has been asking about you."

"Really."

"He said you haven't called him since the dinner."

"I've been busy. I'm working six nights a week now."

"At this little mystery job?" Shawn rolled his eyes at his little sister. He didn't understand why she just didn't come to the firm with everyone else. It was a family business. They could always find something for her to do.

"It's not a mystery job."

She's About That Life: Familiar Territory – Keisha Elle

"Why won't you tell anybody where you work? Maybe I want to stop by and take my sis to lunch or something?"

"I would always make time for lunch with you Shawn. All you have to do is call and I will be more than happy to meet you somewhere."

"What's really going on? There's just something different about you sis. You've been really secretive lately. You stay away all the time and it's hard for anybody to get in touch with you."

"I just have other things going on Shawn." She looked down at sleeping Xavier, hoping that Shawn would stop with his accusations.

"I hope that's all sis." He looked around, peeping the uncomfortable gazes of both Kat and Jace. He changed the tone of the conversation. "David's having a dinner

She's About That Life: Familiar Territory – Keisha Elle

Saturday night to officially announce his candidacy for Judge. He would…We would love for you to come."

"I'll try my best."

The ringing of her phone made baby Xavier jump. He instantly began crying, upset that he was woken from his peaceful sleep. The private number infuriated Asanti. Who the hell was calling her? Asanti stood up, passing her nephew to his mother. She lightly hugged Kat before doing the same to Shawn.

"Are you leaving?" Shawn asked.

"Yes, I got a lot to do at home before Komiko gets back tonight."

"I understand. I'll call you tomorrow."

"That sounds good."

Asanti walked over and wrapped her arms around Jace in a loose hug. She whispered in his ear.

"I'll be over at seven."

She's About That Life: Familiar Territory – Keisha Elle

Jace didn't respond. He didn't have to. They both knew that he would be home and ready before the specified time.

Asanti gave one last wave to everyone before exiting the door. She was settled in her car and ready to pull out of her parking space when her phone rung once again. Pissed off, she put the car in park and slid the green phone icon across the screen, answering the call.

"Hello!"

"It's good to hear your voice."

"Who is this?"

"News travels fast you know. It took me awhile, but I finally tracked you down. To my surprise, I found out you're shaking your ass for the highest bidder."

"Who is this?"

"So you thought you were just going to leave me? You didn't think I would find you?"

She's About That Life: Familiar Territory – Keisha Elle

Asanti thought hard before realizing the identity of the person on the other line.

"Justin?"

"That's right baby. It's me. I hope you're ready. I'll be in Atlanta soon to claim what's mine."

Chapter 13

Justin was still on her mind when Asanti knocked on Jace's door thirty minutes after seven. She drove around for several hours trying to clear her mind. She couldn't understand how the hell he found her. Although she kept the same number after leaving without warning, he never called. She assumed that he conceded without a fight. That was her mistake. Not only did he know that she was in Atlanta, he knew that she was a dancer. Besides the club workers, Komiko, and now recently Sidney, no one knew her little secret.

Justin had a tempter and Asanti knew firsthand that he wasn't the one to play with. She witnessed him smack the shit out of his son's mother with her own eyes. Monique told him that he was not allowed to see his son and he wasn't having it. He smacked her so hard that Asanti was positive that people around the world felt the

245

impact. When Monique recovered and stood up from the floor, clinching her bleeding mouth, she changed her tune. Justin and Asanti left with Justin Jr, and Monique didn't complain one bit.

This would have been enough to turn most women off. The possibility of one day saying something to tick Justin off and being handled violently remained in the back of Asanti's mind. He was different with her though. Besides some name-calling and a few choice words, Justin was not the abusive monster he portrayed toward others. In fact, he was gentle. The way he played with her hair when they laid in bed together, or how he massaged her entire body before making her scream out his name was evident of that. If it wasn't for his wandering eyes, Asanti would still be in Louisville, right by his side.

Jace answered the door with a contagious smile. He had changed from his earlier dark Polo shirt and crisp

She's About That Life: Familiar Territory – Keisha Elle

jeans, to a white tee and sweats. Even dressed down, he was sexy as hell.

"I thought you changed your mind," Jace said, referring to Asanti's late arrival.

"Sorry about that."

"You're here now. That's all that matters." Jace stepped aside, allowing Asanti to enter.

She was amazed by the décor. His apartment screamed, simple, but expensive. It was her first time inside Jace's apartment and although she didn't take him for a neat freak, it was apparent that he was. The thick cushions were perfectly placed on the matching toffee colored sofa and love seat. A black handmade throw blanket rested comfortably across the sofa, while numerous black and toffee accent pillows filled both the couch and loveseat. Two large black suede accent chairs completed the seating arrangement, which sat atop a thick black area rug covering

She's About That Life: Familiar Territory – Keisha Elle

slate tile floors. A gas fireplace lined by feaux rock panels

sat in the middle of one the dark tan walls. Random

artwork, which must have cost a fortune, covered the

others. A black wall clock in the shape of a stop sign sat

close to the front door. Asanti wondered if it was his subtle

way of telling his guests when it was time to go.

"You have a nice place here."

"Thank you. Would you like a tour?"

"Why not."

Asanti followed an eager Jace through an open

doorway leading to the large kitchen. He was more than

happy to show what his hard work had afforded him. Her

eyes zoomed in on the stainless steel appliances and granite

countertops. The room was absent of the typical large,

bulky stove and oven combination. Instead, a stainless steel

double oven and smooth cooktop gave the kitchen an

upscale appearance. Every dish, pot, and eating utensil was

She's About That Life: Familiar Territory – Keisha Elle

covered behind cherry wood cabinets. The kitchen looked

as if it had never been used. An island sat in the middle of

the room, acting as a divider between the kitchen and the

dining room. A large dual sink sat in the middle of the

island. Asanti thought Komiko's kitchen was nice, but this

was on another level.

A half bathroom sat just right off the kitchen. An

alternate entry was possible through the far end of the

living room. In addition to the usual toilet and sink, a large

brass enclosed oval mirror was affixed to the navy blue

wall, right above the sink. A small black table with a clear

vase and colorful lilies sat in one of the corners. On the

back of the toilet was a small basket of potpourri that

invaded Asanti's nostrils as soon as the door was opened.

The door was closed shortly thereafter.

She's About That Life: Familiar Territory – Keisha Elle

Asanti followed Jace down a long hallway. He stopped to open the door to a moderately sized bedroom. Asanti stuck her head into the room and looked around.

"This is my guest room."

"Do you have guests often?" Asanti asked the question, but it came out more accusatory than an actual question.

"Not overnight. This room has never been used."

He pointed to a closed door on the opposite side of the hall.

"This is a full bathroom." He didn't even open the door. Instead, he continued down the hall as Asanti followed.

The hallway stopped at a set of closed French doors. He looked over his shoulder, making sure that Asanti was behind him before opening them. What Asanti saw, was not what she expected.

She's About That Life: Familiar Territory – Keisha Elle

The room was massive. It made Komiko's apartment look like a one-car garagage in comparison. A large King size platform bed rested comfortably against in the wall. Besides a separate sitting area, with a couch and small table, a large seventy-inch television sat mounted on the wall. The oversized room was plain. So much more could have been done with the area. The white walls were absent of pictures, paintings, or artwork. There were no clocks, no calendars, nothing relating to time.

"You have a lot of unused space in here." Asanti said walking around. She was already contemplating what she would do if the space was hers.

"It's a bedroom. It's where I lay my head."

"Still, you need some color."

Asanti walked over to the bed, running her hand over the thick white Italian comforter. It was soft to the

She's About That Life: Familiar Territory – Keisha Elle

touch and matched the White Italian drapes opened on both of the room's windows.

"I'm not in to all that." Jace said honestly. "Maybe if I had you here with me, I'd consider redecorating."

Asanti blushed, her cheeks turning the same rosy red color as her belted romper. She turned, noticing an opened door and headed in its direction. Jace was right on her heels.

She entered his huge master bathroom. The large garden tub was big enough to seat at least three people comfortably. A separate shower with glass doors stood alone a few feet away. The left side of the 'his and her' sink was occupied with his personal hygiene products. The right side was bare. The toilet was in a small room with its own door. A mirrored sliding door was at the far end of the bathroom. Asanti slid it open and walked right into a huge walk-in closet. It was big enough to be considered a small bedroom.

"Wow. You have your own store in here."

Every shelf was filled with a variety of different shoes. Suits, slacks, and shirts hung from hangers. A shelving area inside the closet contained his socks and ties.

"When you look good, you feel good right?" Jace asked following behind Asanti.

"I guess."

"Have you decided what you want to eat?"

"Is pizza okay with you?" Asanti asked, retreating from the master bathroom and making her way back to the living room. She took a seat on his plush sofa.

"Yeah, that's cool. What kind do you want?"

"Whatever you get. I'm not picky."

Jace smiled and retrieved his phone from his pocket. He tapped on the screen a couple times before

She's About That Life: Familiar Territory – Keisha Elle

raising the phone to his ear and placing his order. When he was done, he took a seat on the sofa next to Asanti.

"The food will be here in about thirty minutes."

"Okay." She could feel his eyes burning a hole right through her. She turned away, avoiding his gaze.

"What are you doing Saturday?"

"Working."

"What time are you getting off?"

"I'm not sure. Why?"

"Everyone at the firm is going to David's dinner. I was thinking maybe we could go together."

"As in a date?"

"If that's what you want to call it, yeah."

She heard about her father's dinner from Shawn, and now Jace was asking her to be his date. David was her father. He didn't even pick up the phone and tell her about it himself. Even though they weren't really speaking, this

She's About That Life: Familiar Territory – Keisha Elle

was an important time in his life. She would have preferred a personal invitation from her father.

"I'm pretty sure I won't be able to make it. Saturday nights bring out the best tippers."

"What do you mean?"

She knew she had fucked up once the question left his lips. She thought fast, trying to find a way to dig herself out of the hole she just created.

"I didn't mean it like that."

"How did you mean it?" His voice became serious. He adjusted his position on the couch. "The only people I know that get tips on a Saturday night are waitresses and strippers."

Asanti swallowed hard, not knowing what to say. The disappointed look on his face told her that he had already had an assumption.

She's About That Life: Familiar Territory – Keisha Elle

"Are you a stripper Asanti?" He got right to the point. "Do you take your clothes off for money?"

"Where is this coming from?"

"You work at night, you won't tell anyone where you work, you just said you get tips. I've seen the car you drive and the bags you come with. I guarantee you couldn't afford that shit on a waitress' salary. Please, tell me you're not a stripper."

"I'm not a stripper."

Jace visibly relaxed.

"So what do you do?"

Asanti looked Jace square in the eye as her lie rolled off her tongue.

"I'm a bartender. I make drinks and I get tips."

"A bartender?" He eyed her suspiciously. "Why would you keep that a secret?"

"Because. I don't want to be a disappointment."

She's About That Life: Familiar Territory – Keisha Elle

"I don't understand." He moved closer to her.

"My father is one of the best lawyers in the state. He's about to run for judge. Shawn is a lawyer. Sidney is in school to be a lawyer. Hell, even Cynthia went to law school, even though she doesn't practice now. Then there's little ole' me." She wiped a stray tear from her eye. "Everyone around me is successful. I know my father would be ashamed if he knew what I did for a living. He hoped that I would be more than what I am."

Jace kissed Asanti softly on her cheek and ran his fingers through her hair.

"Are you happy with what you do? If so, it doesn't matter what anyone else thinks."

"That's the thing. I'm not." More tears escaped and Jace softly wiped them away. After her run-in with Sidney, Asanti had been thinking a lot about her life and the choices she made. She didn't want to dance anymore.

She's About That Life: Familiar Territory – Keisha Elle

Although she enjoyed the luxuries that dancing afforded her, she knew she couldn't do it forever. She thought about the Master's degree program that she walked away from. The what-ifs started clouding her mind.

"So what are you going to do about it?"

"I don't know."

Knock. Knock.

Jace stood up and walked toward the door. It hadn't been thirty minutes yet, but he was starving. He dug in his pocket to retrieve some cash, but when he opened the door it wasn't the pizza and wings that he ordered. Instead, it was Raven.

"Hey. What are you doing here?" Jace guiltily blocked her entrance. From her position on the couch Asanti could not see who was at the door, but she clearly heard a female's voice.

"Are you going to let me in?"

She's About That Life: Familiar Territory – Keisha Elle

"I kind of have company right now. What's up?"

"It's Friday night silly. If we leave now we can bypass the evening crowd. They should be gone by the time we get there."

"Oh shit, I forgot. Maybe tomorrow night. No wait, we got the dinner tomorrow. Let's do it Sunday."

"No, we're going tonight. As your workout partner, I am not listening to your excuses. Now go get dressed. I'll wait for you." She pushed past his sad attempt at blocking the door and walked in to see Asanti sitting comfortably on the couch. Asanti rose to her feet quickly.

"Am I interrupting something?" Raven asked, looking Asanti up and down. She wasn't expecting to see another woman in his home.

"Raven, this is Asanti." Jace quickly stood between the two women.

She's About That Life: Familiar Territory – Keisha Elle

"We've met." Raven offered a fake smile. "How are you hun. Were you about to leave?"

"No, I wasn't. As a matter of fact, we're waiting on our food." Asanti returned Raven's intense gaze.

"Really? Jace, what's going on?" Raven finally turned in his direction. "Is this the reason why you haven't been answering my calls?"

Asanti turned her attention to Jace as well. She wanted to know the answer to that question. Was she being played?

"Raven, chill!"

"I will not chill Jace. I thought we were taking things slow, trying to work things out. Now, you're here with her. I can only imagine what you two have been doing."

"What are you taking about? We've never talked about working things out. Where did you get that idea?"

She's About That Life: Familiar Territory – Keisha Elle

"What have we been doing the past six months?" Raven's attitude went from zero to a ghetto real quick. "You know I want you back. I fucked up and I know I did. I thought we were on the right track."

"Maybe I should leave." Asanti didn't want no part of that fight. Jace obviously had more on his plate than he could handle.

"No, stay." Jace grabbed Asanti's wrist and pleaded with his eyes.

"No, let her go. We need to talk about this."

"Talk about what Raven? Where the hell is this coming from? I've never given you the idea that we were anything more than friends. We're coworkers. That's it."

"No, that's bullshit."

"You're fucking crazy Raven. I don't know what's going into you, but this ain't the Raven I know standing in front of me."

She's About That Life: Familiar Territory – Keisha Elle

Raven ignored his comment, turning her attention right back to Asanti.

"So, is he fucking you yet?"

"Raven that's enough." Jace objected.

"She's a grown woman Jace. She can speak for herself."

"That's none of your business." Asanti finally spoke up.

"Raven, you need to leave, now!"

"Fine, but this isn't over Jace Rainwater."

Raven stopped just as Jace was opening the door. She turned on her heels and looked in Asanti's direction.

"You know, there's a girl named Duchess who looks just like you." A devilish grin appeared across Raven's face. "She works at Club Fantasy. They say everyone has a twin, she's definitely yours." With that last comment, she walked out of Jace's door as he slammed it hard behind her.

All the color drained from Asanti's face. Like Sidney, Raven also knew her little secret. She didn't know why Raven had it out for her. Was it because of Jace? Raven had ruined the entire evening with just a few words. Asanti was no longer hungry. She wanted to get the hell out of there and fast. She didn't want to risk Raven coming back and exposing her little secret.

"I think I should go."

"The food isn't even here yet. Don't leave."

"Komiko should be in any minute now. I still have some cleaning up to do."

"Asanti, please don't let her ruin our evening. Things were going great before she got here. I apologize for her interruption."

She's About That Life: Familiar Territory – Keisha Elle

"It's not that," Asanti lied. "I really do need to get going. I'll call you."

Jace didn't persist. He watched Asanti let her own self out. He stood in silence as the door closed behind her, wondering what he did wrong.

She's About That Life: Familiar Territory – Keisha Elle

Chapter 14

The sound of beating against her wall woke Asanti up from her sleep.

"Yes." A faint female voice moaned. "Right there."

Asanti wiped her eyes thinking that she must be dreaming. When the banging continued, she knew she wasn't dreaming. She rose up from the bed, her naked body instantly chilled after removing her warm cover. Grabbing her robe, she left her bedroom to investigate the noise. As she neared Komiko's room, the banging increased. Usually when Komiko came home, she would wake Asanti up. Not this time. From the sounds coming from the room, she was getting some good loving.

Asanti inched closer to the partially open door. She could see clearly through the two-inch crack. Rico was hitting it doggy style, gripping Komiko's hair tightly. It looked as though her neck was going to snap back, but the

She's About That Life: Familiar Territory – Keisha Elle

moans that came out of Komiko's mouth, were filled with pleasure. The headboard repeatedly banged against the wall until Rico quickly ejected his erect pole, and changed positions.

He stood, wrapping his arms around Komiko's small waist and lifted her in the air. Her long legs wrapped around his waist. He quickly inserted himself again. She bounced up and down on his stiff cock, screaming out in delight in the process.

"Oh Rico," she moaned, her arms around his neck for support.

"That's right baby."

"Harder. Fuck this pussy." Her voice was just above a whisper.

Rico did as he was told, pounding her harder as the slapping noise of her body hitting his on each downward thrust increased.

She's About That Life: Familiar Territory – Keisha Elle

Asanti watched intently, both jealous and turned on at the same time. Jealous that Komiko was getting dicked down like she was, and turned on that Rico was putting it down so well. The tickling feeling between her legs indicated her horniness. She, like Komiko, wanted to feel something stiff between her legs.

Rico slowed his pace when his eyes met Asanti's. She was busted, peeping at them through the cracked door. Komiko threw her head back, enjoying the slow strokes. Rico eyed Asanti cautiously, but didn't stop. He gave her a wink, letting her know that he knew she was there.

Asanti retreated from the door just as Komiko breathily requested him to pick up the pace.

"Faster, baby faster." Komiko begged.

Asanti was both embarrassed and ashamed when she entered her bedroom and closed the door. She thought she was going to be getting the same treatment from Jace

She's About That Life: Familiar Territory – Keisha Elle

when she arrived at his apartment just the day before, but after Raven's sudden arrival, she was left feeling deprived and horny.

She reached for her cell phone, noting that it was just after 2AM. She dialed Jace's number, hoping she didn't wake him.

"Hello."

"Are you sleep?"

"Not yet. What's up?"

"Open the door."

Asanti ended the call, preventing him from questioning her further. Power walking to the front door, she opened it quickly to see Jace leaning against his opened door. He wore a pair of gray sweatpants. She could see the black elastic from his boxer briefs. His shirtless chest showed off his toned abs. He smiled when she closed the door behind her and entered his.

She's About That Life: Familiar Territory – Keisha Elle

The pair stood quiet, not saying a word. The unspoken chemistry was enough to ignite a fire of its own. Jace broke the silence first.

"I'm glad you're here." His eyes skimmed the length of her, hoping she was naked underneath her thin robe.

"Are you?"

"Of course. You left in a hurry last night. I didn't know what to think."

Asanti grabbed her robe's belt, loosely tied at the waist. She untied the weak knot, allowing the robe to fall open. Jace's initial assumption was confirmed. Asanti's naked body teased him through the opening. He inhaled deeply, his body full of anticipation.

"You didn't try to stop me." Asanti opened the front of her robe allowing it to slip over her shoulders and fall to the floor.

She's About That Life: Familiar Territory – Keisha Elle

Jace watched intently. His stiffening dick appreciated the beautiful, naked woman standing in front of him.

"I should have." Jace licked his lips and rubbed his hands together. "That's my fault, but you're here now."

Jace stepped closer, instinctively drawn to her . Asanti stepped back, not ready for Jace to devour the treat that she had already made up her mind she was going to give him. Instead, she made her way through his apartment, remembering the path leading straight to his bedroom. When she entered it, she carefully climbed on top of his bed, making sure that he got a good glimpse of her jiggling ass crawling all fours.

Jace stood in the doorway smiling, understanding Asanti's game. She was teasing him. This was a game he was definitely going to play.

She's About That Life: Familiar Territory – Keisha Elle

She spread her legs wide, resting one hand comfortably behind her head and the other slowly making its way to her creamy middle. Her fingers found her clit, circling around it, before dipping inside her wet hole.

"Umm," she moaned, enjoying the pleasure she was giving herself.

Jace stroked himself through his pants, unable to hide his excitement. Watching Asanti enjoying the feel of her own hands exploring her body only made Jace want her more. When she extracted her fingers and placed them in her mouth, Jace couldn't resist. He walked to the edge of the bed, watching her slurp up the last remnants of her wetness from her fingers.

"My turn." He cupped his hands around her hips, pulling her closer to the edge.

He lowered himself to the floor and positioned himself in between her opened legs. He trailed small kisses

She's About That Life: Familiar Territory – Keisha Elle

on the inside of her thighs, inhaling the scent of her sweet aroma. When his tongue found the entrance to her opening, he licked it softly, parting her lower lips slowly with his fingers.

He flicked his tongue across her clit, enjoying Asanti's soft moans. Licking and softly sucking, his mouth quickly filled with her warm juices. He swallowed them up, burying his head deeper between her legs. Taking her clit in his mouth, he sucked hard, almost bringing her to an instant orgasm. She wrapped her legs around his head, trapping him right where she wanted him. Jace sucked harder, ready to feel Asanti's body tremble against his face. When her legs tensed, momentarily suffocating him in her wetness, he latched onto her clit tightly. Her orgasm was quick, but satisfying. She released her grip as Jace slowly freed her clit from his mouth, devouring her juices as if he hadn't ate in days.

She's About That Life: Familiar Territory – Keisha Elle

"Oh my God," Asanti said in a breathy tone. As usual, Jace didn't disappoint.

Jace stood slowly, wiping his face. Asanti repositioned herself on the bed, ready to give the same treatment to his erect dick. She laid on her back, her head hanging off the bed. Jace stood over her, his dick inches from her open mouth. He inserted it slowly, and Asanti went to work, giving up the neck pussy without hesitation. She damn near swallowed his dick whole. Her gag reflex was non-existent as all ten inches slid easily down her throat. She bobbed up and down, making slurping noises in the process. The sight of his thick dick down her throat and Asanti's messy head game was too much for him to handle. He hated busting quick, but he couldn't control himself. She was that good.

"Baby, I'm about to cum."

She's About That Life: Familiar Territory – Keisha Elle

Asanti didn't stop. She continued her quick pace taking his entire length in her mouth, releasing it, and slurping it right back up. His body stiffened, his cum quickly making its way to the tip. Jace tried to eject his dick from her mouth, but Asanti used her hand to hold it in place. Jace busted hard, right in her mouth. His warm load exploded in the back of her throat. She milked him dry, swallowing each drop.

"Damn girl," was all he could manage to say.

Asanti wasn't done yet. Although they both got off individually, now, it was time to get it together. Asanti made her way to her knees, wrapped her arms around Jace's neck and kissed him passionately. He didn't resist. She leaned backwards, lowering herself onto the bed, taking Jace with her. Still embraced in the kiss, she reached for his dick, gradually making its way back to its maximum length.

She's About That Life: Familiar Territory – Keisha Elle

"Put it in."

Jace didn't hesitate. He quickly found her wet hole and slowly inserted himself. He made love to her missionary style, looking deep into her eyes with each slow stroke. Asanti moaned in delight, feeling both physically and emotionally complete. She loved Jace and watching him make love to her was something that she would never get used to. He maintained his slow pace, expelling himself until the head was almost out, only to insert it again. Her moans turned him on. Asanti had always been more than a friend to him and being inside her was the best feeling he had ever felt. He was gone off her, wishing that she would be his forever. An overwhelming feeling of emotion overcome him through each precise thrust.

"I love you baby."

"I love you too." Asanti responded quickly, moving her hips to Jace's rhythm.

She's About That Life: Familiar Territory – Keisha Elle

"I want to be with you and only you." Jace's tone became breathy as his second nut began to rise. "I love you Asanti. Oh…Baby, I'm about to cum."

Asanti placed her hands on Jace's ass, guiding him deep inside her. She felt her own orgasm building up, turned on by his deep strokes and his loving words. This was the man she wanted to be with and he felt the same way about her. They came together, trembling and holding each other tightly.

Jace rolled off her slowly. They laid said by side without saying a word. For the first time in their lives they both had what they wanted – each other.

She's About That Life: Familiar Territory – Keisha Elle

She's About That Life: Familiar Territory – Keisha Elle

Chapter 15

Asanti took a deep breath before taking a step inside the house. She was two hours late, and knew that her father would be disappointed. She had been sexed by Jace so good that she didn't want to stop. They laid in silence for half an hour before Komiko's knocking sent them both racing toward the closet, searching for something to wear.

Jace stood by her side, his arm looped in hers. Her hip hugging dress and steady stride beamed confidence. With her man, by her side, nothing could go wrong. Komiko followed, a few steps behind. Her floor length ivory evening gown slowly dragged behind. Rico watched his step, making sure that he didn't become tangled in the extra material.

The living room was filled with rich, well-dressed guests laughing and chatting amongst themselves. Asanti felt out of place around some of the city's most elite, but as

She's About That Life: Familiar Territory – Keisha Elle

the eye candy on Jace's arm, it was something she needed to get used to.

Asanti scanned the large room, hoping to find a familiar face. She saw Shawn's wide smile heading in her direction.

"I'm glad everyone made it. You missed dinner, but David has been putting off making his announcement hoping that you would show up." He kissed Asanti and Komiko both on the cheek and gave Jace and Rico dap. "He's going to be happy to see you."

Everyone followed Shawn through the house, to the back yard. The perfectly manicured lawn was filled with dozens of white tables and chairs.

The staff was beginning to clear the tables and put the food away. Asanti didn't realize she would miss the entire dinner. Ever since her father became a lawyer, he no

She's About That Life: Familiar Territory – Keisha Elle

longer followed 'colored people' time. If he said dinner was at six, dinner started at six – no exceptions. Asanti didn't think the entire dinner would start and conclude without her.

Shawn led them to the furthest table on the green lawn. David, Cynthia, Sidney, and Raven all sat in deep conversation. The smile on Cynthia's face disappeared when she saw Asanti approaching. Sidney and Raven's eyes turned cold.

"Asanti!" David smiled wide as he stood to greet his daughter. It had been some time since the two had seen each other.

"Hi dad."

When he wrapped his strong arms tightly around his daughter, Asanti didn't protest. She welcomed the embrace without wanting the moment to end. When he slowly released his grip, she grabbed his arm and held on tight. He kissed her on the forehead and extended his arm to shake Jace and Rico's hand. Komiko gave him a light hug, adding Asanti to the mix. With Asanti possessively holding on to her father, it would have been impossible to pry her off of him.

"You all are just in time. I was about to get everyone together to make my big announcement. Most of the crowd has already made their way inside." David pointed to the food being packed up and put away. "There's not much left, but if you're hungry, you all can grab something quick."

"We're fine." Most of the food was already put away and she didn't want to inconvenience the staff by making them pull everything out again. Everyone played along, declining the food being offered.

She's About That Life: Familiar Territory – Keisha Elle

Cynthia stood and joined her husband at his side. Regardless of how Asanti felt, she was the main woman in his life.

"David, honey, it's about that time. Are you ready?" She rubbed her husband's tight chest through his shirt.

David looked at his watch, noting that it was almost eight o'clock.

"Yes. Everyone, follow me inside. I'm about to make my announcement."

Asanti released his father's arm as Cynthia grabbed hold of the other one greedily.

"It's nice to see everyone." Cynthia scanned over Rico, Komiko, Jace, and finally Asanti. "The dinner was phenomenal. Chef Helmsley really outdid himself. Maybe next time you'll get here on time and enjoy the meal like everyone else."

She's About That Life: Familiar Territory – Keisha Elle

That last comment was directed at Asanti. Cynthia was convinced that she was the cause of the tardiness. Once again, she was only thinking of herself.

"Mom, they're here. That's all that matters." Shawn spoke up, reminding everyone of his presence. "Let's all just go inside. I'll go get Kat and tell her to come down."

"Where is Kat?" Cynthia asked, not realizing that she hadn't seen her for some time.

"She went upstairs to put the baby to sleep. It was too noisy out here."

David led the way with his wife following at his side. Everyone looked at each other and followed behind. Asanti made a mental note to stop and get something to eat once this shindig was over.

They were half-way to the door when the sound of Asanti's name rang out.

She's About That Life: Familiar Territory – Keisha Elle

"Asanti!" Sidney's voice called from behind her. "Wait. Can I talk to you?"

Asanti wished she hadn't halted when she heard her name being called. If she had kept going, she probably could have played it off.

"What do you want?" She turned around and snapped.

Sidney and Raven caught up with the group in five long strides. Sidney stood, smiling from ear-to-ear. She enjoyed the uncomfortable look spread across Asanti's face. Her lack of direct eye contact made the situation all the more fun. Asanti was at her mercy, and now it was time to let the games begin.

Raven mean-mugged the entire group, still upset that Jace had dissed her the way he had. Jace damn near ignored her at work, only speaking to her when it was

She's About That Life: Familiar Territory – Keisha Elle

absolutely necessary. She had to find a way to get back into his life, and more importantly back into his bed. It made her blood boil just thinking about Asanti being with Jace. In her mind, he was her man. The gossip that Sidney recently shared with her was going to be the demise of Jace and Asanti's relationship, and Raven couldn't wait to see the fireworks.

"Jace, is she always like this?" Sidney questioned, her lips slowly turning into a smile. "She's so quick to snap at me. It's like she's a different person. I should name all of your multiple personalities. I think I'll call this one Duchess."

Rico loudly cleared his throat. As the owner of the club and one of Jace's close friends, he had become entangled in Asanti's web of lies. Everyone looked in his direction and he slowly smiled it off. Even with the attention momentarily shifted, a lump still formed in Asanti's throat. Her life as she knew it was about to come crumbling down.

"Don't start Sidney. Tonight is about David."

Jace's deep voice was intoxicating. Although she had a thing for him in the past, the feeling was long gone. She had to admit though, he was even more handsome now, than he was back then.

"You're right Jace. I just wanted to talk to Asanti. That's all."

"You have an ulterior motive for everything that you do. What do you want?" Asanti asked.

"Just see what she wants. We'll be inside when you're done." Jace leaned in close and gave Asanti a kiss on her cheek. He wanted to give Asanti privacy while the women talked. He nodded in Sidney and Raven's direction

She's About That Life: Familiar Territory – Keisha Elle

before entering into a conversation with Rico and Komiko as they headed toward the house. Asanti looked on, wishing someone would save her. She had no such luck. When her crew was out of earshot, Sidney began.

"How long do you think you're going to keep this game up?" Sidney asked, her arms crossed in front of her small chest. The strapless black dress that she wore fit snugly against her small, square frame.

"I don't know what you're talking about."

"Don't give me that. You shake your ass for money and God knows what else. I should go and tell Jace right now. He should know what kind of woman you really are."

Sidney took a few steps in the direction of the house. Raven was right on her heels. Asanti's pathetic voice stopped her dead in her tracks.

"Don't."

She's About That Life: Familiar Territory – Keisha Elle

"Speak up. What did you say?" Sidney heard the pitiful plea, but wanted to add insult to injury and make Asanti repeat herself. She was in control and calling all of the shots.

"I said don't." Asanti hung her head low.

"It's not good for me to start the habit of withholding information. What kind of lawyer would that make me? Better yet, what kind of woman would that make me?"

Raven giggled at her friend's sarcasm. She had been standing quiet, enjoying the show playing out in front of her. Sidney had everything under control and she didn't even have to say a word.

"Let's stop with the mind games Sidney." Asanti's voice became serious. "You obviously want something from me. What is it? What do you want in exchange for you keeping your mouth shut?"

"Hmmm...Well, what do we want Raven?" Sidney appeared to be in deep thought before rolling her eyes. The two friend's eyes met and they both burst out laughing in unison.

"You think this is a game? You think this is fucking funny? I don't have time for this shit." Asanti turned to walk away. She was not going to entertain the situation any longer. She would just have to find a way to stop Sidney herself.

"There is something you can do."

Asanti stopped mid-stride and turned her attention back to the women. They were whispering amongst themselves. After a pregnant pause Sidney spoke up.

"I want you to leave. Leave and never come back."

She's About That Life: Familiar Territory – Keisha Elle

"And how am I going to do that? I just can't up and leave."

"If you want to keep your little secret a secret, you will leave. And to send you on your way, I have a surprise of my own."

"I don't like surprises."

"Don't worry, you'll love this one." Sidney walked past her, a cold look plastered on her face. She intentionally bumped into Asanti with her shoulder. Raven repeated the gesture.

Asanti was dumbfounded. What did Sidney mean? How was she going to get out of this situation? She could still hear the girls laughing as they walked away. Her body instantly filled with rage. Who the hell did Sidney think she was? She was going to pay. She didn't know how she was

She's About That Life: Familiar Territory – Keisha Elle

going to do it or what she was going to do, but Sidney was going to get hers.

*****

"Good evening everyone. Thank you for joining my family and I in celebration tonight. It has been my pleasure to host this event and I am grateful to be surrounded by my friends and family.

I have been a resident of this great city for almost twenty years. I moved here to pursue a career in law and Emory University gave me the tools needed to be a successful attorney. In my time here, I have had the chance of meeting people both in and out of the courtroom. I have litigated some complex cases, but I have always stayed true to my beliefs. I understand the laws and made it my passion to help serve the community in which I reside.

She's About That Life: Familiar Territory – Keisha Elle

The citizens here have a strong tradition of electing competent, honest, and fair judges, and I plan on carrying on that tradition. I am officially announcing my candidacy for circuit clerk judge. I pledge to follow the law and make a positive impact within the city that I have grown to love. Again, I thank you for joining my family and I tonight. I ask that you continue to support me and my campaign to ensure that the right person for the job is elected into office. Thank you."

A roar of applause filled the large room. Words of encouragement were shouted from all different directions. Before long, David was bum-rushed with people congratulating him on his candidacy. Many expected him to run years ago. Not only did he have a successful practice, he was also very popular within the community. With him on their side, his clients were almost guaranteed to win.

She's About That Life: Familiar Territory – Keisha Elle

The loud doorbell was barely audible over the talking crowd. Cynthia left her husband's side to answer the door. Asanti stood filling Komiko in on Sidney's treats and Raven's flunky behavior, while David and Shawn entertained David and other colleagues from the office. Rico had excused himself to the bathroom minutes prior. He was taking a long time. Komiko didn't complain. She knew that he was probably checking up on business, using the excuse that he had to go to the bathroom.

Asanti kept her eye on Sidney. Every now and then, Sidney would wave in Asanti's direction. The gesture pissed Asanti off even more.

When Cynthia returned a few minutes later, Asanti's heart stopped in her chest. All the color drained from her face. She stood as still as a statue, not believing her eyes. There stood Justin, scanning the room as if he was

She's About That Life: Familiar Territory – Keisha Elle

looking for someone. His blue jean shirt and shorts set was at least two sizes too big. He walked wide legged to keep the pants from falling down. His eyes were unreadable.

"There she is," Cynthia mouthed, pointing in Asanti's direction. She was irritated that Asanti had the nerve to invite a thug to such an important event.

Justin was on her before she had time to escape.

"Hello beautiful." He wrapped his arms around her waist and pulled her close. "You act like you ain't happy to see me."

Justin leaned in for a kiss, but Asanti leaned in the opposite direction.

"Justin, what the hell is wrong with you. What are you doing here?"

"I came to claim what's mine."

She's About That Life: Familiar Territory – Keisha Elle

Asanti tried to escape his embrace. She wiggled out of his waist grip, only to have him grab her arm tightly.

"So you thought you could just leave me?"

"Take your fucking hands off of her." Komiko commanded, watching Asanti's face grimace in pain. "You take your fucking hands off of her right now, or…"

"Or what?" Justin cut her off. "Mind your own damn business." He back-handed her so hard that she fell backwards.

The commotion caught Jace's attention. He quickly walked over to check things out. When he saw Asanti punching wildly with one arm and Komiko slowly regaining her balance, he put two and two together. He couldn't contain his own rage.

Without a second thought, he cocked his hand back and punched Justin, landing a solid right to his chin.

She's About That Life: Familiar Territory – Keisha Elle

The blow stung, and for a moment, Justin saw stars. He was never the one to back down though. He had lost many fights in his time, but he always made sure his opponent looked just as bad, if not worse than he did. He just needed a few seconds to regain his composure. With her wrist still tightly gripped with his hand, he moved Asanti in front of him. She became his human shield.

"Let her go." Jace watched intently, waiting for Justin to slip up and turn at a different angle. He was sure that he could bypass Asanti's pretty face and still land a nice blow.

"Who the fuck are you?" Justin tightened his grip on Asanti's wrist.

"I said, let her go."

"Look my dude, I don't know who you are, but this here," he used his free hand to point himself, then Asanti, and back to himself, "doesn't concern you. This is my bitch and I'll do whatever the fuck I want to her."

Asanti swung violently with her free hand. Justin was going to let her go or he'd have a couple of nice sized bruises as souvenirs.

"You're crazy. I am not yours anymore. Get off of me."

The opportunity arose and Jace took it. Without warning, Jace stuck him, hitting him square in the jaw with his closed fist. The impact caused him to release Asanti's wrist as he fell back onto a large vase filled with colorful flowers. It broke on impact.

"Oh my God. Someone call the police." One of the guests yelled, witnessing the brawl ensuing.

"They're fighting." Another high pitched voice yelled.

She's About That Life: Familiar Territory – Keisha Elle

The guests scattered to the perimeter of the room like roaches. Several cell phones placed calls to 911 in fear of the situation getting even more out of hand.

Justin recovered quickly, throwing a few punches of his own in Jace's direction. His aim was not as good, but he made contact, momentarily stunning Jace. Before he could hit Jace again, David was in the middle of the two mean.

"Young man, you need to leave." David's voice was deep and serious. He didn't know who the hell this man was coming in and causing a mockery of his candidacy announcement, but he wasn't going to tolerate it any longer.

"If I go, she goes." Justin pointed to Asanti.

Jace lunged for him, ready to give him a serious beat down. He stopped when his face came inches away

She's About That Life: Familiar Territory – Keisha Elle

from the 9mm handgun that Justin pulled from under his shirt.

"He's got a gun! Oh my God. He's got a gun!" a male voice echoed in the distance.

Guests began exiting the door like a stampede. The fear alone gave even the slowest guest lightning speed.

"Nobody else better fucking move." Justin barked.

David held his hands up, determined not to let anything happen to his baby girl.

"I don't know who you are, but you have a room full of lawyers and a few judges here. You better think long and hard about your decision young man. I've asked you nicely to leave my home. Now I'm telling you. Get the hell out of here and don't come back."

She's About That Life: Familiar Territory – Keisha Elle

The sound of the nearing police vehicle gave Justin something to think about. He knew he couldn't take on everyone in the room. One wrong move, and the tables could easily be turned. He looked at Asanti, standing behind the man who had caused the swelling of his jaw. He was going to fuck them both up. Right now was just not the time. Estimating that he had just enough time to get away, he high tailed it out of there without a second thought.

"Are you okay?" David asked his daughter, nursing her sore wrist.

"Yes dad, I'm fine."

"Once again, you found a way to ruin this night." Cynthia's voice was cold. "You invite a thug with a gun to my home. What if something had happened to David? What if one of the guests were hurt?"

"I…"

She's About That Life: Familiar Territory – Keisha Elle

"I, nothing! Asanti you bring trouble everywhere you go!" Cynthia was over it.

"I didn't invite him."

"Well, how did he get here?" David questioned.

"I don't know. I haven't seen him in months. He just called my phone out of the blue one day." Asanti tried to recall the details of the conversation, but she was too shaken up. "I never planned on any of this happening." She turned to her dad. "I'm sorry. I'm so sorry."

"You got that right." Cynthia barked. "You are sorry. A sorry excuse for a human being."

She walked away with a look of disgust on her face. David shook his head. He opened his mouth to speak, but turned away and followed his wife. He was really disappointed with his daughter.

She's About That Life: Familiar Territory – Keisha Elle

Komiko wrapped her hands around Asanti's shoulders.

"I'm sorry sis."

Asanti leaned in, accepting Komiko's embrace. She looked up at Jace, his expression unreadable.

"Did you invite him here Asanti?" Jace asked.

"No, why would I do that?"

"You didn't tell me about him calling. When were you going to tell me that? Why are you keeping secrets from me?"

"I'm not. I just didn't think it was a big deal. I didn't think he would show up here and cause a scene."

"Well, he did. Right in front of a group of your father's peers. I bet this is going to make front page news." He ran his hand over his wavy hair. "I need some air."

She's About That Life: Familiar Territory – Keisha Elle

Asanti knew that that meant. He was mad. Mad at her. She just couldn't understand how Justin found her, let alone know where her father lived. She never introduced him to any of her family. Her mind was baffled as she tried to make sense of the situation.

She caught a moving figure out of the corner of her eye. She turned, watching Sidney smile in triumph. Raven sat beside her grinning from ear-to-ear. Almost on cue, Sidney raised her hand and waived. She smiled when Asanti's face began to show signs of understanding. Sidney was the mastermind behind Justin's arrival. What Asanti didn't know was that Sidney was far from done. She had even more tricks up her sleeve.

She's About That Life: Familiar Territory – Keisha Elle

She's About That Life: Familiar Territory – Keisha Elle

Chapter 16

Asanti paced back and forth in an upstairs bedroom. The commotion had died down, and the embarrassment that she felt made her want to grab all her shit and leave. She was tired of running. Once again, she had disappointed her father and ruined his night at the same time. Even though it wasn't her fault, she was guilty by association, and that was something she had a hard time accepting. She had to explain to her father that she did not plan Justin's arrival, nor did she anticipate for him to act a damn fool.

Private calls rang back to back on her phone. She pressed the red phone icon ignoring each and every one of them. It didn't take a rocket scientist to figure out who it was. Justin had already ruined her evening. She was not going to spend any of her time entertaining his foolishness..

"Can I come in?" Rico asked, stucking his head in the half-open door.

She's About That Life: Familiar Territory – Keisha Elle

Rico's neat dreads were pulled back from his face. He was handsome in his fitted shirt and slacks, a much more sophisticated look from his usual khaki pants and Polo shirt.

He entered before she answered his question.

"Look Duchess...My bad, Asanti." He corrected himself. "I'm sorry about the way things played out. I know you're really feeling my man and I hate to see you like this."

"Like you care." Asanti snapped, not wanting to hear the bullshit rolling off his tongue. "You could care less about me or what I'm going through. All you're worried about is how much money I bring into the club."

"I didn't come in here for your attitude and that's not true. Komiko thinks of you as a little sister. So that kind of makes us family."

She's About That Life: Familiar Territory – Keisha Elle

"Don't say anything to me about family. Family don't keep secrets. Komiko is my girl. She's the only person that I have here besides Shawn and Jace that really give a damn about me. Now you're in here talking to me about family. If she knew the truth, she wouldn't think of me as family and you know it."

"Chill out girl. Keep your mouth shut and I'll do the same. I'm not trying to jeopardize my relationship with Komiko."

"You have some nerve Rico. Have you told her about Diana and the baby?"

"Did you tell her how you were on your knees sucking my shit? Did you tell Jace that you're my top money maker? Of course not. Don't ask me a stupid question like that. I don't even know if that baby is mine."

She's About That Life: Familiar Territory – Keisha Elle

"So you did sleep with her?" Asanti stopped pacing the floor. "That's some foul shit Rico. Komiko doesn't deserve that."

"I don't want to hear that shit. You're no saint and this here ain't about me. Like I said earlier, I didn't come in here for no attitude."

"So what did you come in here for?"

"I just want to make sure you're okay. Every day you perform, there's a packed house. I don't want anything distracting you from work. When you get money, I get money. I've invested a lot in you, and we've both reaped the benefits. I plan for that to continue. I want you to know that I have resources. I'm not gonna stand by while a pussy nigga throws you off your game. I have a whole army of faithful niggas in my corner. If you need this situation handled, just say the word and its done."

She's About That Life: Familiar Territory – Keisha Elle

Asanti caught on to his drift. He was giving her a way out.

"You'll handle Justin?"

"Say the word and its done."

Asanti ran her hand over her forehead. With Justin out of the picture, she wouldn't have to worry about him popping up ever again. She could go about her life without looking over her shoulder. He had never been violent towards her before, but the look on his face when he possessively grabbed her arm told her that at that moment, he didn't give a fuck. That's what had her over the edge. The fear of the unknown had her mind racing.

"I don't want anything bad to happen to him." Asanti said honestly. She took a seat on the queen size bed.

"You can't be serious. That nigga came in here on a mission. He probably would have tried to fuck you up if my boy didn't step in. He put his hands on my girl and that shit ain't gonna fly."

"I know." Asanti truly felt bad about Komiko. She didn't have anything to do with it, but Justin still took his rage out on her. "I'm going to handle it. I just have to wait for the right time. When everyone has cooled off a bit, I can try to talk to him and clear up any confusion."

"Fuck that! What's really going on Asanti? Do you still have feelings for this dude?"

"No!"

"So what's the problem then. He started a war and I'm going to finish it. Jace would do the same shit for you. He was ready to go toe-to-toe with that clown. Do you know how that looks for a lawyer to be involved in some shit like that? I'm not gonna let my man risk his reputation on this bullshit. He fucked up when he put his hands on my girl. His ass needs to be taught a lesson and I'm just the one to make that happen."

Asanti lowered her head, trying to hide the tears slowly making their way down her face. For so many years she stood by Justin. Through the infidelity, she remained by his side. He never pushed her to be a better person like Jace had. Instead, he kept her comfortable so that she would always have to rely on him for everything. After stepping away, the blindfold was removed from her eyes. He was not the man that she thought he was. She wanted more. She deserved more. That realization didn't help the fact that for all those years, she loved him. Rico intervening was just not an option.

"I'll handle it Rico."

"You do that," Rico said, heading back towards the door. "Just know that he's on borrowed time. When I catch up to him, it's lights out. No questions asked." With that, he disappeared into the hallway.

Asanti released her curl-filled up do, allowing her curls to fall freely. The interaction with Rico combined with the stress from earlier made her head hurt. Wishing she could redo the day over, she walked to the window, hoping the sunset would be her calming force. She was in her zone, searching for peace and tranquility when Sidney's voice yanked her back into reality.

"This day just keeps getting better." Sidney closed the door behind her. "You and Rico? Wait until Jace hears about this."

"Fuck you!" Asanti yelled out in a panic. It was the only thing that she could think of as her mind tried to piece together what was happening. She was busted. By the look on Sidney's face, she was loving every minute of it.

She's About That Life: Familiar Territory – Keisha Elle

"Now it all makes sense. You work for Rico and you're putting in work *with* Rico." Sidney laughed. "Is that how you're keeping him quiet? Sucking his dick on command?"

"Whatever Sidney." Asanti walked past her preparing to make an exit of her own. She was not in the mood to deal with the bullshit.

Sidney grabbed her arm, halting her exit. Asanti snatched it out of her grasp defensively.

"Don't fucking touch me. As a matter of fact, I would stay the hell away from me if I was you."

"My, my, my... Where did this violent streak come from? Is that something you learned on your knees or shaking your ass? Is this what you're going to teach that bastard baby of yours?"

She's About That Life: Familiar Territory – Keisha Elle

The image of her once pregnant belly popped in her head. She stopped thinking about her child shortly after the miscarriage. She pushed it as far back in her mind as she could. The mention of a baby brought back all of those emotions. Asanti couldn't control her anger. She had heard enough. She slapped Sidney hard across her fast, leaving an instant red hand print. Before Sidney had time to react, Asanti was on her, hitting her so hard that it sent her to the floor. Asanti maintained the upper hand, positioning herself on top of Sidney, punching at her face and pulling at her shoulder-length hair.

"Stop! Stop it right now!" Asanti felt her body being pulled off of Sidney. She used her legs to get a few last kicks in. When she finally turned to see whose strong arms were grasping her tightly, she swallowed hard as her eyes met her father's gaze.

She's About That Life: Familiar Territory – Keisha Elle

"What the hell is wrong with you? Asanti, I just don't understand you lately."

Asanti shut down, thinking about all of the times she had been reprimanded as in the past. She couldn't possibly tell her father the truth.

"David, I've been telling you this for years." Cynthia appeared out of nowhere, running to the aid of her daughter. "That girl is evil. She's like a ticking time bomb. She acts like she's on drugs or something."

At that very moment, Asanti wished she did have some drugs. The way she was feeling, she could do an 8-ball of coke by herself. It would numb everything she was currently feeling and put her on cloud nine. Hidden in her closet, in an old shoe box, was just what she needed. She would hit up that spot once she got home.

She's About That Life: Familiar Territory – Keisha Elle

"It's okay mom. I'm okay." Sidney licked her bottom lip, tasting blood. She was playing down the situation like she always did, in turn adding fuel to the fire. "She's just angry right now."

"No, it's not okay. Stop defending her actions!" Cynthia turned to Asanti, wanting her to know exactly how she felt. She wanted her to know that this was the end. "I accepted you with open arms. I can't take it anymore. You have serious issues. I don't want you back in this house. You are a danger to everyone around you and I truly feel sorry for anyone who entertains your nonsense."

Asanti turned towards the door, seeing Shawn, Jace, Rico, Komiko, and Raven all standing in the doorway. Asanti turned her attention to her father, wanting him to say something. He said nothing. Her phone buzzed, ending the awkward silence that crept upon them. It was Justin, calling

She's About That Life: Familiar Territory – Keisha Elle

from a private number again. Enraged, she threw the phone down on the floor. It separated into several pieces.

"You see David. Something is wrong with her!" Cynthia blurted out, watching Asanti stomp on her phone with her stiletto heels. "She's not stable."

"You're not fucking stable!" Asanti snapped. The pile of shit that she just fed everyone only infuriated Asanti even more. "You wanted your happy little family, and I was never part of that picture. Every time you get mad, that's the first thing that comes out of your mouth. You want me to leave."

David cleared his throat, hoping to neutralize the situation.

"Asanti, you need to calm down." He turned to his wife. "No one is going anywhere. Let's talk about this like adults."

She's About That Life: Familiar Territory – Keisha Elle

"Look at my child David. She attacked her like a savage dog. If you think I'm going to sit here while she justifies her violence, you and her both have another thing coming."

"Dammit, I am so tired of this shit!" David swore loudly, silencing everyone in the room. He rarely used profanity. When he did, people knew that he meant business. "I know she needs help, and family helps their own. Making her leave does not change the situation."

Asanti turned in Sidney's direction. She palmed the left side of her face with her hand, which showed signs of swelling. Asanti almost felt bad for hitting her the way she did. When an evil grin appeared on her face, all sympathy previously felt for her was thrown out the door.

"I'm out of here." Asanti began her stride towards the door. Whoever was in her way needed to clear the path

She's About That Life: Familiar Territory – Keisha Elle

fast, because she had no intent of stopping to ask them to move.

"If you walk out that door, you're turning your back on your family!" David yelled, tired of his daughter running when the situation become uncomfortable. He wanted to get to the bottom of Asanti's crazy behavior lately. The only way to do that was to talk to her and find out what was going on. "We can go somewhere private if you need to. I am worried about you Asanti."

"Don't bother," Asanti said, preparing to say something that she knew would hurt her father to his core. "I've never felt like I was a part of this family anyway. Today just confirmed it. You and your wife can have the perfect life that she so desperately wants. You don't ever have to worry about me again."

She's About That Life: Familiar Territory – Keisha Elle

Asanti walked to the doorway. The look of complete shock filled everyone faces. Her eyes met Jace's. He reached his hand out toward her, but she ignored it. Right now, she just needed her space. Everyone parted like the Red Sea, giving Asanti the space needed to exit the room. Raven stood firm, blocking her exit. Without warning, Asanti pushed past her, knocking her hard into the door panel. Asanti's heels clicked loudly down the wooden steps. Before long, the only sound that could be heard was the slamming of the front door. Asanti was gone, and she never intended to come back.

She's About That Life: Familiar Territory – Keisha Elle

Chapter 17

"Call me and let me know how everything goes." Komiko said, smoothing a stray strand of Asanti's hair out of her face.

Asanti looked up, watching Jace stand in his doorway, waiting for her to enter.

"I will sis." Asanti kissed Komiko on her cheek and entered Jace's apartment.

Jace walked over to his couch and sat down. Asanti followed, taking a seat beside him. He began talking once she was situated in her seat.

"I don't even know what to say to your right now."

"I know." Asanti sighed loudly. "And I'm sorry. Today did not go as planned."

"That's an understatement." Jace removed his shirt, revealing a white t-shirt underneath.

She's About That Life: Familiar Territory – Keisha Elle

"Jace, I know things look bad, but everything was just blown out of proportion."

"You invite another dude to your dad's house. The same mother fucker shows his ass in front of everyone. Next thing I know you're fighting with Sidney. What part of that was blown out of proportion?"

"I didn't invite him."

"How did he know you were there? Why would he just show up like that?"

Asanti was quiet. Jace took her silence as a sign of guilt.

"I thought we were trying to make something happen. You got me looking like a damn fool. You're still talking to this dude."

"It wasn't like that."

She's About That Life: Familiar Territory – Keisha Elle

"How was it then? What am I missing? Cause right now, things don't look too good on your end."

"I don't know why he was there."

"You don't know?"

Again, silence.

"Asanti, I told you from day one I'm not with the games. I've been honest with you. For you to just sit back and lie to me is not cool. If this isn't what you want, fine. Just be a woman about it."

"This is what I want."

"Start talking then."

Asanti took a deep breath. It was now or never. She had to tell Jace the truth, or risk losing him for good. She didn't know how he would take the news, but she knew it would be best to hear it from her instead of someone else.

She's About That Life: Familiar Territory – Keisha Elle

"Justin started calling me last week."

Jace faced her. He wanted to look into her eyes as she spoke. If she was lying, her face would give it all away. He didn't say a word.

"I didn't know it was him at first. He called my phone private. I didn't answer it. He never left any voicemails. The calls continued. Finally, I answered the call. I wanted to find out who kept calling me."

Asanti looked at Jace's tight face. His expression was serious. She continued.

"When I answered, he basically told me that he was coming to get me. He said some other stuff too, but I kind of brushed it off."

"Why would you do that?"

She's About That Life: Familiar Territory – Keisha Elle

"I didn't think he knew where I was. He never met my dad. I didn't know that he would actually come here and show up at my dad's house."

"How did he know where David lived?"

"Sidney." Asanti spoke softly and held her head low.

"How the hell does Sidney play into all of this?"

"I don't have concrete proof," she said, her tone increasing in intensity. "But I know she did. I know she's the one that sent him there."

Jace's patience was fading fast. The words coming out of Asanti's mouth didn't make sense.

"I thought you would keep it real with me, but I see you can't." He walked over to his door opening it. It was

She's About That Life: Familiar Territory – Keisha Elle

his way of telling her it was time to go without having to say the actual words himself.

Asanti let him stand there while she attempted to gain the courage to open her mouth and let the truth fall out. She couldn't find it. When she didn't move, he shifted his weight to his other leg, letting her know that he was growing tired. She still didn't move.

"Asanti, we're not going to do this."

"Jace, I don't want Justin. I like what we're building and I wouldn't do anything to jeopardize that. Sidney is the one trying to ruin things."

"This has nothing to do with Sidney. This is between you and me."

Asanti rolled her eyes. Sidney had everyone convinced that she was so innocent. Asanti knew differently. She knew how much of a conniving little bitch she could be.

"She has you all hypnotized. She's turned everyone against me, including my dad. She's trying to do the same with you. Think about it Jace? Why would I send Justin to my father's house when you were going to be there? Even if I was trying to be dirty, which I'm not, that's a little sloppy, don't you think?"

Jace thought about her words. It did seem a little shady. Closing the door, he returned to his position on the couch next to her.

"I want to believe you. I deal with people every day lying to my face and expecting the outcome to fall in their favor. I can spot that shit a mile away. I know you're not telling me the full story. I can see it in your eyes. The only

way this relationship is going to work is if you're
completely honest with me. What are you not telling me?"

"I know it looks bad."

"Tell me something I don't know."

"If you knew everything, I guarantee that you
wouldn't be sitting here right now."

"Try me," he challenged. He was ready to hear any
and everything.

A soft knock at the door saved her. Jace didn't
move. His eyes were still fixed on her.

"Are you going to get that?" She asked, feeling his
intense gaze on her.

"It's not important."

"You never know." Asanti stood up quickly, happy
to break the staring contest going on between them.

She's About That Life: Familiar Territory – Keisha Elle

She looked out the peephole, watching Komiko draw her fist back for another knock. Asanti quickly opened the door.

"Rico and I are stepping out for a bite to eat. As soon as I stepped in the door, my stomach started growling like a wild animal."

Asanti smiled at Komiko's perfect timing. From his position in the apartment, Jace could not see Komiko give Asanti a wink. Komiko's visit wasn't just a coincidence.

"Wanna go?" Komiko asked stepping into the apartment. Rico was right behind her. "It's getting late, but I'm sure we can find a spot still open."

"Sure." Asanti was all for anything that would get her out of that uncomfortable situation.

"Jace?" Rico called out, looking in Jace's direction.

She's About That Life: Familiar Territory – Keisha Elle

"Have fun. I'm going to chill right here."

"Come on Jace. Don't make your girl a third wheel. I got some stuff to run by you anyway. You know, legal shit with the club."

Jace knew his friend well, and knew what he was doing. Still the attorney in him couldn't let the 'legal' word slip out of his friend's mouth without exploring further.

"Alright, I'm coming."

"Let's take two cars." Komiko chimed in. "I want to talk to my girl." Komiko looped her arm in Asanti's. "We'll follow you," she said before she walked out the door, arm and arm with her best friend.

*****

"What are you going to do?" Komiko asked following behind Jace's glossy Range Rover.

She's About That Life: Familiar Territory – Keisha Elle

"Girl, I don't know. The truth will almost guarantee he'll leave."

"You can't keep going on like this. Sidney is bound to open her big mouth, and when that happens, all hell is gonna break loose."

"I don't have any other options right now. That's just a chance I'll have to take. I just need more time sis. I need to tell him in my own way."

"I don't think that's a good idea. This can end badly for everyone." Komiko followed Jace into an empty Waffle House parking lot.

They found themselves in a small booth situated beside a large window. They placed their orders after briefly reviewing the plastic menu. Everyone had a healthy appetite, and it reflected in their food selections.

She's About That Life: Familiar Territory – Keisha Elle

"How's business going?" Komiko asked Jace, taking a sip of her water.

"Busy. I think David and my dad may have bitten off more than they can chew."

"How so?" Komiko questioned.

"They need to hire another attorney. We're all working long hours to just to keep up our current clientele. We're short staffed, but those two will never turn down money. Sometimes I just don't think there's enough time in the day to get everything done." He took a sip of his Coke. "I'll be leaving next Friday to meet with another potential client in Savannah. If we don't get help soon, I don't know how we can manage to keep everyone satisfied."

Asanti turned in his direction, surprised. This was her first time hearing of this.

She's About That Life: Familiar Territory – Keisha Elle

"When were you going to tell me you were leaving?"

"I found out yesterday," he said, returning her gaze. "I was going to make it a day trip, but I thought I'd drive the extra two hours and visit one of my frat brothers in Jacksonville. I haven't seen Aaron in years."

"Aaron?" Rico asked. "Aaron Jackson?"

"Yeah."

"Big A! What's he been up to?"

"He joined the navy after college. He's been in Jacksonville for four years now."

"No man, I didn't. We lost touch after college. Next time you talk to him, tell him I asked about him. Slip him my number and tell that nigga to call me."

She's About That Life: Familiar Territory – Keisha Elle

"Are you busy next weekend? Come to Jacksonville with me."

"Saturday is all bad. It's Baller Night. I already got some big names scheduled to come through. If everything falls into place, they'll be spending some big money too! I got to stay behind to match sure everything goes smoothly."

Asanti sat frozen in her seat, all the color drained from her face. A couple days before, Rico mentioned Baller Night to her. It was a night he had twice a year, where only the high rollers came through to show love. Strippers from all over, migrated down south for a chance to dance for some of the wealthiest people around. He limited the roster to fifteen girls and five backups. Asanti was his first choice. She immediately agreed after finding out how much money was at stake. Now, she sat watching him talk to Jace about the very same event that she would be shaking her ass at.

"Damn." Jace said, putting his elbow on the table and resting his chin in his palm. "I didn't realize it was next weekend. I can go see Aaron another time. You know I'm always down to support."

The blank expression on Asanti's face transferred to both Rico and Komiko. They finally figured out why Asanti looked as though she was about to pass out at any minute. Rico had just as much too loose as Asanti if Jace showed up and saw what Asanti really did for a living. Rico thought fast, quickly excusing Jace from his event.

"Naw man, go see Aaron. I appreciate the support, but you can see tits and ass at my spot any day."

Two young, blonde waitresses arrived, placing various plates on the table. They smiled when everyone had

She's About That Life: Familiar Territory – Keisha Elle

their correct food selections, and dismissed themselves after asking if there was anything else that they could do.

Everyone ate in silence, enjoying the fresh breakfast selections they had ordered. With their hunger was satisfied, Komiko was the first to spark up a conversation.

"So Asanti, what are you going to do about that nutcase Justin?"

Asanti used a napkin to wipe her mouth. She gave Komiko a 'did you just ask me that fucking question' look. She didn't want to get into this now.

"I don't know." She answered honestly. "But I'll figure something out."

"You better." Rico added. "That mothafucka is on borrowed time. He better hope our paths never cross again. What kind of man puts his hands on a woman?"

She's About That Life: Familiar Territory – Keisha Elle

"Asanti I don't know what you saw in him. He's not all the way there."

"Sis, he wasn't always like that. I feel like I'm partly to blame."

"Why is that?" Jace asked, breaking his silence.

"I'm not innocent in all of this. I did a lot of things that I'm not proud of."

Asanti swallowed hard before divulging specifics of her complicated relationship with Justin. She honestly answered any question thrown her way. She told them about Justin's cheating, her miscarriage, and even how she left Louisville without so much as a forwarding address. Jace wrapped his arm around Asanti's shoulders. He hated seeing his girl so full of hurt emotions. It made him hate Justin even more.

She's About That Life: Familiar Territory – Keisha Elle

"Why do you think Sidney had something to do with him coming here?" Jace asked.

"I never told Justin about the miscarriage. A few days after I was released from the hospital, I found the DNA results. I left the same day. When I was arguing with Sidney at my dad's house, she brought up my baby. The only person who knew I was pregnant was Justin. He had to have told her."

Jace thought about what Asanti's words. Was it possible that Sidney could be so malicious? Jace didn't want to think that she could be. As Asanti continued to speak, the probability of Sidney being responsible for this entire ordeal was increasing.

"I don't know how she did it, but I can almost bet I know why. She's trying to ruin me. I don't understand why no one else sees it. She's joined forces with Raven and

She's About That Life: Familiar Territory – Keisha Elle

they're trying to make my life a living hell. Raven wants you back, but you already know that."

Jace didn't respond. Instead, he returned her gaze, not knowing what to say. Trying to ease the mood, Asanti explained how her chance meeting with Komiko turned into a sisterhood.

The foursome tipped the waitress lovely and started their quest back home. They returned to the same cars they rode in. Asanti used the time to talk to Komiko. She shared her fears of Sidney exposing her to Jace. Komiko, trying to be the voice of reason, urged Asanti once again to tell Jace the truth. Asanti took everything Komiko said into consideration, but deep down, she already knew that it would be over once Jace found out – regardless of who told him.

She's About That Life: Familiar Territory – Keisha Elle

When the cars were parked, everyone quickly exited and entered the apartment building, boarding the elevator to the seventh floor. Komiko and Rico quickly entered Komiko's apartment. Jace and Asanti stood in the hallway, not wanting to leave each other's side, but not knowing what to say either. Asanti broke the awkward silence.

"Jace, maybe I should go home tonight."

"Why?"

"I think its best."

"I don't want you to."

"Jace, I can tell that you have a lot on your mind. I want to give you the space you need. I'll come over tomorrow if you're up to it."

Everyone seemed to be on decent terms when Rico and Komiko left. Asanti didn't want to take any chances.

She's About That Life: Familiar Territory – Keisha Elle

She headed towards Komiko's door, expecting to go back home and let the information divulged to Jace marinate overnight. He stopped her before she turned the doorknob.

Jace wrapped his arms around Asanti's slim waist.

"I'm not mad at you, I'm made at the situation." He turned her around and lifted her chin. He wanted to look deep into her hazel eyes. "I love you and I only want what's best for you."

A lone tear escaped Asanti's eye. Jace wiped it away. He kissed her deeply and she eagerly accepted his tongue. At that moment she knew everything would be okay.

Jace grabbed her hand, leading her into his apartment and straight to his bedroom. He slowly removed her clothes before doing the same to his own. He made love to her, allowing his body to become one with hers. Inside

She's About That Life: Familiar Territory – Keisha Elle

her was where he wanted to be. He remained there until his body couldn't take it anymore. They shared an intense orgasm, each one holding on to the other tight, while their orgasmic high slowly dissipated. Jace's limp dick slid out at a snail's pace. Asanti welcomed his seed buried deep inside her. She loved him and the way he made love to her, she knew he loved her too.

She's About That Life: Familiar Territory – Keisha Elle

Chapter 18

"Rico, I'm done. I can't do this anymore." Asanti said, sitting across from Rico on his infamous white leather couch.

Asanti sat with her thick legs crossed. Her appearance was much more calm and laid back than usual. Her natural ringlets hung free, while her t-shirt and jeans kept everything covered. Rico leaned back in his chair and ran his hand across his forehead.

"Can't do what?"

"This." She pointed around the room. "Be here. Dancing. I can't do this anymore."

"Think about what you're saying?"

"I have. I've thought about it long and hard. I don't like lying to Jace about where I go every night."

She's About That Life: Familiar Territory – Keisha Elle

"What if you just cut back, you know, just do a couple nights a week?"

"Come on now Rico, don't make this harder than it already is. I'm walking away from a lot of money."

Through her short stint dancing, Asanti learned a lot and met a lot of people in the process. She had regular customers who frequented the club just to see her. She had a steady cash flow, thanks to the generous tips that she received. Unlike most dancers, Rico didn't charge Asanti the usual 'house fee.' Every penny that she made was hers. When Rico found out that she was messing with his boy, he didn't feel right taking money from her, knowing she was trying to get on her feet. In a way, he felt he was taking from Jace. If it were anyone else, he wouldn't have cared. He made more money off the numerous drinks Asanti convinced each of her customers to buy.

She's About That Life: Familiar Territory – Keisha Elle

"What can I do to make you re-consider?" Rico was desperate.

There was no way he could find a replacement of her caliber on such short notice. Some women studied hard to master their craft, while others were just born with it. Asanti fell in the latter category. She was born to dance. She had a presence that stopped everyone in the room. Whenever she was on stage, all eyes were on her. Her pretty face and curvy frame accented her natural stage presence.

"My mind is made up. I promised you I'd perform at Baller Night and I'll keep my promise. After that, I'm done. Tomorrow is my last night."

"Duchess, I need you."

"Asanti. Call me, Asanti. After tomorrow night, Duchess will be dead and buried. We both need this, much

She's About That Life: Familiar Territory – Keisha Elle

more than you're willing to admit. You have just as much to lose as I do."

"We've made it this far. Sidney hasn't said a word. Justin hasn't been around. They're both all bark and no bite. Just give me enough time to find someone to replace you."

"I can't do that."

Asanti stood, preparing herself to exit the room. She could see the frustration painted on Rico's face. Although she appreciated him taking a chance on her, she knew that her time was up. She was ready to take the confidence learned from her alter ego Duchess, and apply it to her everyday life. She had grown since walking into the doors of Club Fantasy. Dancing was never a permanent option for her. Instead, she used it as a stepping stone toward financial stability. What she learned was that everyone and

She's About That Life: Familiar Territory – Keisha Elle

everything had a price. The price of losing Jace forever was not one that she was willing to pay for without a fight. She had to leave it all behind and find a way to keep Sidney from opening her big mouth.

Asanti left the room, closing the door behind her. Rico didn't say a word as he watched his money walk out the door. She headed down the long hallway to the dressing room, happy to escape the tense situation. She was just about to turn the knob and enter to the dressing room when the mention of her friend's name halted her in her tracks.

"Her name is Komiko." Diana said in a low tone. "She's the reason Rico doesn't want anything to do with me or the baby."

Asanti crept closer to the door. She wanted to make sure she was hearing correctly. Positioning her back against the cold concrete wall, she listened intently.

She's About That Life: Familiar Territory – Keisha Elle

"Tell her the rest," Selena chimed in.

"Check this out. She's friends with Duchess." Diana's tone was cold. Asanti could imagine her talking with clinched teeth. It's something she often did when she was mad.

"Wait? What?" Envy's voice asked confusingly.

"Yes." Selena began. "That bitch is as fake as they come."

"I can't believe this shit. She's supposed to be our girl!" Envy exclaimed.

"With friends like her who needs enemies?" Selena asked without expecting a response. She lowered her voice before continuing. "She better watch her back. Diana is like a sister to me. I don't appreciate that two-faced bitch treating my sister like that."

She's About That Life: Familiar Territory – Keisha Elle

"You're damn right." Envy added. "Fuck Duchess and her little friend too."

The footsteps making their way down the hall caused Asanti to jump. Trying to play off her obvious eavesdropping, she walked away from the door, down the opposite end of the hall. She planned on stopping by and chopping it up with her friends for a while. She wanted to tell them her plans to put dancing to rest. After hearing them talk shit about her with her own ears, she decided against it.

Walking out the back entrance to the club, she climbed in her car and began driving. She didn't have a particular destination. She just needed to clear her mind. Selena's words played back in her mind, 'She better watch her back.'

She's About That Life: Familiar Territory – Keisha Elle

Asanti rode with the window down. The cool night breeze hit the nape of her neck as her ringlets jumped around wildly. She rode around for hours, stopping only once to empty her bladder. After riding out her nearly full tank of gas, she arrived back at her apartment building. Komiko was laying on the couch, watching television when she entered.

"Hey!" Komiko said, raising her head to eye level. What are you doing here?"

"I live here."

"I know that," Komiko said, returning her head to its comfortable resting place. "I just thought you'd be staying over at Jace's place."

"I didn't want to be alone. He left this morning."

"Just admit it. You missed me." Komiko smiled widely, showing off her beautiful white teeth.

She's About That Life: Familiar Territory – Keisha Elle

"Of course I did sis."

Asanti playfully smacked Komiko on the arm. When she attempted to do it again, her vibrating cell phone stopped her. Jace's name appeared across the screen. She answered it quickly.

"Hello."

"Hey baby. I wanted to hear your voice before I called it a night."

Asanti blushed, her body temperature instantly climbing two degrees. Jace's voice alone had the ability to send her to the point of no return.

"Aww…" Asanti cooed. "I miss you."

"I miss you too baby. What are you doing?"

"Nothing, just chillin' with my girl."

Komiko rolled her eyes at Asanti's comment.

She's About That Life: Familiar Territory – Keisha Elle

"Whatever. Go on with that lovey dovey shit."
Komiko didn't want to hear it. As bad as her pussy was
thumping, she hoped Rico would do a surprise pop-up.

Asanti picked up a firm accent pillow and threw it
in Komiko's direction. Komiko turned her head at just the
right time, causing the pillow to land on her right shoulder
before falling to the carpet below.

"Hello." Asanti said raising the phone back to her
ear. She lowered it for the playful exchange with her friend.

"Sounds like you're having fun." Jace said,
referring to the loud bursts of laughter he heard in the
background.

"I was just messing with Komiko." Asanti walked
towards her bedroom for privacy. "Are you on your way to
Florida?"

She's About That Life: Familiar Territory – Keisha Elle

"No, not yet. My meeting took longer than expected. I'm still in Savannah."

"Where are you staying?"

Jace picked up on Asanti's concerned tone. He wanted to ease her mind.

"Chill out girl. I got a hotel room. I'm out of here after I get some sleep in."

"Call me before you leave." Asanti glanced at her wall clock. It was almost 2:00AM.

"I will baby. Have a good night. Think about me."

"Always. I love you Jace." Asanti said softly.

"I love you too."

Asanti sat on her bed quietly, thinking about what had become of her life. She had so many dreams and aspirations. Currently, none of her plans had fallen in place.

353

She's About That Life: Familiar Territory – Keisha Elle

Never in a million years would Asanti have thought that she would be in Atlanta, stripping nonetheless. In a few more hours, it would be a thing of the past. She was going out with a bang.

Asanti found her way to her nightstand. She opened the bottom drawer and removed a few books. Underneath it all, she pulled out a small stash of white powder. She made up her mind that when she left her erotic lifestyle behind, the small drug habit that she developed would be gone as well. She no longer needed the powdery substance to put her in the mood to entertain strange men. Asanti thought about flushing the cocaine down the toilet. She scratched that idea. Turning the knotted clear plastic bag upside down, she watched it settle towards the bottom like an old fashioned sand timer. The thought of one last euphoric high overwhelmed her. It wasn't long before the bag was untied and her acrylic nail dipped in. Cupping a small sample with

She's About That Life: Familiar Territory – Keisha Elle

her nail, she brought it to her nose. Closing off the airway

to her right nostril, she sucked hard with the left. It was

instant gratification. Two more quick hits and her body was

feeling right. She was preparing for another hit, when

Komiko's frantic voice rang in her ear.

"Asanti! Asanti!"

Asanti scrambled to retie the bag and place it back

in the drawer. Her sense of balance was off, but she found

her way back to the living room.

"What?" Her feet were moving so fast that she

almost ran straight into the couch.

"Look! It's my commercial. I'm on TV!"

Asanti turned her head just in time to see Komiko

stand up from a barstool in her designer dress and slowly

walk away. The commercial was for a new draft beer with

the tagline, 'Real women drink beer too.'

She's About That Life: Familiar Territory – Keisha Elle

"I heard it was out, but it's my first time seeing it." A wide smile appeared on her face.

"That's great," was all Asanti could manage to say. Her attention was more on her drugs stashed away in her nightstand.

"Is that all? I thought you'd be happy for me."

"I am." Asanti slurred.

"Are you okay?" Komiko asked, noticing Asanti's change in demeanor.

Komiko's questioning face evoked emotions that Asanti couldn't control. Instantly, tears fell from her eyes. Her drug-induced state brought upon feelings of guilt and sadness.

"I'm sorry. I'm not a good friend."

She's About That Life: Familiar Territory – Keisha Elle

"What are you talking about? You're my best friend."

"No, I'm not. Friends don't do you like this. Friends are honest and don't hold anything back."

Confusion filled Komiko's face. What was Asanti talking about? She wasn't sure if Jace said something to knock her girl off her rocker or not, but Asanti wasn't making sense.

"Is this about the commercial?"

Asanti raised her head to meet Komiko's gaze. The same girl who opened her home up to a complete stranger. She helped her find a job, and had been nothing but nice. Asanti couldn't let Rico keep taking advantage of her trusting heart.

"Rico got another girl pregnant."

She's About That Life: Familiar Territory – Keisha Elle

"What did you just say?"

The realization of what just spilled out of her mouth quickly sobered Asanti up. Her high was blown when tears began welling in Komiko's eyes. There was no turning back now.

"I didn't want to be the one to tell you this, but Rico has been messing with one of his dancers. Her name is Diana, and she's pregnant."

She's About That Life: Familiar Territory – Keisha Elle

Chapter 19

Sitting behind the wheel of her black BMW, Asanti pulled the remainder of her cocaine out of her large tote bag. Digging in quickly, she took each of the last five hits in rapid succession. The back of her throat instantly numbed. Her body quickly relaxed. She was on cloud nine and ready to put Duchess to bed for good.

Asanti thought about her earlier conversation with Komiko. She had been the shoulder to cry on when Komiko poured her eyes out over Rico. He had betrayed her in the worst possible way. Even after the explosive news, Komiko agreed to keep quiet about she knew. She didn't want to put Asanti in the middle of things. This was between her and Rico. She would hold this information in until her friend was no longer employed at Club Fantasy.

Asanti glanced down at the clock enclosed in the wood-grain dashboard. It was 9:30PM. She had just enough time to get ready for her final performance. She stumbled out of the car, miscalculating the distance to the ground. The laughs and snickers that followed proved that her misfortune had been seen by others. Asanti didn't care. With her tote over her should, she walked confidently through the packed parking lot.

Big Zeke stood by the door, inspecting every patron that entered. He smiled when she saw Asanti walking past the long line of people waiting to enter. He motioned her forward with his hand.

"Hey Duchess. You ready for tonight?"

"I stay ready." Asanti said, flashing a smile.

"I hope so. It's a packed house already. Lots of money to be made."

She's About That Life: Familiar Territory – Keisha Elle

Asanti smiled in his direction before entering. The DJ was on the mic, joking with the crowd and offering free drinks for random acts.

"Let's get this party started right!" He yelled. "I know what everybody came for, but I think we got just as much talent in the audience tonight. Which one of you pretty ladies out there wants a drink?"

An average, flat-chested chick with box braids ran up on stage. She tried to shake what her momma didn't give her. Even though she was a good dancer, the absence of the fatty mounds in the back that men liked, decreased the effect. She was booed off the stage without the Green Jolly Rancher cocktail that she wanted.

Asanti passed through the full crowd. The line of men holding up the wall took the building capacity over limit by more than fifty people. One man tried to cop a feel when she passed by. She swatted his hand away. Until he was contributing to her pockets, he needed to keep his hands to himself.

Asanti made her way to the dressing room. Selena and Envy sat in a corner, finishing off a bag of white stuff. Diana sat on the couch talking in their direction. They all stopped when she entered.

"Well look what the cat drug in," Envy said, pinching her burning nostril shut.

"Don't start with me Envy. I'm not here for your shit. I'm here to do my set and be out."

"Fuck you and your set you two-faced bitch," Selena spat. She grew balls as she headed in Asanti's direction. She was ready to throw blows.

She's About That Life: Familiar Territory – Keisha Elle

Diana quickly blocked her path, sensing Selena's true intention. They were closer than close, but Diana wanted to handle the situation on her own.

"Let me handle it," Diana said softly. "This is my problem. I don't want you to get involved."

Asanti dressed as if they weren't in the room. She didn't care what they had to say about her. If any one of them bitches tried her tonight, it would be on and popping.

"Fuck that! I want to beat her ass right now!" Selena was on one.

Asanti pulled her black sheer G-string into its rightful place and faced the trio. She wasn't going to be caught off guard in a possible three on one. She stood with her hands on her hips. She wished a bitch would.

"I got this." Diana's voice was just above a whisper.

She's About That Life: Familiar Territory – Keisha Elle

"Fine." Selena threw her empty plastic bag in the trash can. "I'll see you on stage."

Selena hugged her friend before giving Asanti an icy stare. Envy followed suite and left with Selena. Asanti knew they hadn't gone too far with Diana in the room alone.

"Say whatever you got to say. After that, I don't want to hear it anymore," Asanti said, grabbing a bottle of shimmer lotion for her legs.

"I never thought you would cross me like that. I really thought you were my friend." Diana's timid voice spoke.

"Diana, you…"

"I don't want to hear anything you have to say. You're nothing but a backstabbing liar who never gave a damn about me. You played me for a fool. You knew how I felt about Rico. You knew that I was having his baby."

Diana pointed to her small bulge to add emphasis.

"I didn't know. At first, I mean. I didn't know that you two were messing around. We were friends, but I've known Komiko longer. My loyalty is to her. I didn't know how to tell either one of you."

"Duchess, Rico wants you," New New announced, walking into the dressing room. She stopped when she stepped into the tense atmosphere.

"You couldn't tell the truth if your life depended on it. I hope you get everything you deserve."

Diana brushed past Asanti, grabbing her purse on her way out. She stopped in the doorway, just before exiting.

"I just hope I get a front row seat."

She's About That Life: Familiar Territory – Keisha Elle

Diana slammed the door without hesitation.

"What was that all about?" New New asked, stuffing a wad of bills in her locker.

"You don't want to know." Asanti ran her hands through her long, straightened mane. She shook all thoughts of Diana out of her mind. "Is Rico in his office?"

"No. He's on stage talking to that new cute DJ." New New smiled. "He slipped me a twenty."

Asanti rolled her eyes at New New's comment. The DJ never gave her less than a Benjamin. New New needed to step her game up if she wanted to roll with the big dogs.

She didn't see Rico on stage. Instead, Envy was performing, giving the crowd just what they wanted. Even though she was mad, Asanti couldn't hate on Envy. She was putting on one hell of a show. Taking her eyes off, she examined the large crowd. She noticed a man with his back

She's About That Life: Familiar Territory – Keisha Elle

to her. He was Rico's height and build, with a long ponytail of fresh dreads. She headed in his direction. When he turned to start a conversation with a man to his right, Asanti saw from his side profile that it wasn't Rico. She gave up. She wasn't about to go on an exploration in search of him. If he wanted to talk to her, he would have to wait until after her set.

"Give it up for Envy!" The DJ yelled through the mic when the music stopped. He paused to watch her collect her cash and jiggle her round ass off the stage. "Damn! Did y'all see all that ass? That's gonna be a hard act to follow, but I think I know who can. Ladies and Gentlemen, give it up for Duchess!"

Asanti struggled through the crowd in an attempt to make her way to the stage. It wasn't the entrance she planned, but it would have to do.

She's About That Life: Familiar Territory – Keisha Elle

"Duchess, where are you girl? Don't leave us hanging!" The DJ spat in the mic when she didn't appear.

Stuck behind, two big burly dudes not willing to budge, Asanti searched for an alternate route. She tried to yell that she was coming, but her voice appeared as a whisper in the noisy crowd. Asanti stepped over an empty chair. Its former occupant had moved closer to the stage to get a glimpse of the infamous Duchess. The stage was now in her sight. Scanning for a clear path, her heart stopped when she noticed Sidney and Raven walking her way.

"Duchess, they're calling your name." Sidney teased. "What are you waiting for?"

"Fuck you Sidney!"

Raven disappeared in the crowd. Sidney continued.

She's About That Life: Familiar Territory – Keisha Elle

"Should I call security?" Sidney asked, reaching up and touching one of the rhinestones of Asanti's bra straps. "Are you gonna spaz out and try to attack me again?"

"I'm not dropping to your level tonight." Asanti said, swatting Sidney's hand away. "Jace knows that you sent Justin to my father's house. And you know what? We're still together. There's nothing you can do or say that will change that." Asanti smiled in satisfaction.

"Are you sure about that?" A wicked grin spread across Sidney's face. "When I talked to Jace, I got a different impression."

"You're pathetic. You'll say anything to get under my skin. I don't believe anything that comes out of your fucking mouth."

"I knew you were going to say that." She pointed towards two figures walking in their direction. When

She's About That Life: Familiar Territory – Keisha Elle

Asanti realized that Raven had reemerged with Jace by her side, she panicked. "Why don't you ask him yourself?"

"What's going on?" Jace asked, closing the space between them.

"Jace." Asanti froze. All of the blood rushed from her face. She was sure that her skin was as white as a ghost. "What are you doing here?"

"I was going to ask you the same question." His confused face looked her up and down, noting her bedazzled bra and sheer G-string.

"I thought you were in Florida."

"I thought you were at home."

A spotlight began circling the room looking for its intended target. Asanti opened her mouth, ready to mouth off a lie, but the DJ's voice over the mic stopped her. The spotlight was now on her.

"There she is...working the crowd. Give it up for Duchess!"

Jace stood in silent anger as the crowd migrated to the edge of the room, giving Asanti a large section of the seating area as a make-shift stage. Sidney and Raven watched on in amused satisfaction. They joined the crowd of onlookers watching the show playing out in front of them. Jace's piercing eyes shot daggers straight through Asanti.

"So this is what you do?"

"I can explain."

"No explanation needed. Sidney told me everything. I didn't want to believe it, but I see it with my own eyes." He took a step back. "Don't let me stop you. Go ahead,

She's About That Life: Familiar Territory – Keisha Elle

shake your ass for everybody to see. That's what you like, right?"

"Jace it's not like that."

"Fuck all that talking!" A loud male voice yelled. "I didn't come here for all that. DJ start the music. I want to see how this bitch gets down."

A roar of laughter began. A loud, uptempo beat blasted from the speakers. Men began digging in their pockets, flashing large amounts of cash. They were ready to spend. There was no way in hell she was dancing now; not when her life was falling apart right before her eyes. Disappointment lined Jace's face. He shook his head in disbelief as Asanti took small steps backward. When he turned and walked away in the opposite direction, she tucked her tail between her legs, and ran.

She's About That Life: Familiar Territory – Keisha Elle

She's About That Life: Familiar Territory – Keisha Elle

She's About That Life: Familiar Territory – Keisha Elle

Chapter 20

Asanti ran towards Rico's office. She wanted to warn him about Jace. She wanted him to know that her little secret was exposed. He would probably be hearing Jace's wrath. When his door swung open and Komiko's voiced yelled her obscenities, Asanti knew that shit was about to get much worse.

"Don't fucking touch me!" she yelled. "Don't you ever fucking touch me again."

"Baby." Rico attempted to grab Komiko's arm, but she quickly pulled it away. When he saw Asanti approaching, he re-directed his frustration.

"You're going to believe this bitch?" He pointed in Asanti's direction.

"Leave her out of it. This is between you and me Rico!" Komiko spat.

She's About That Life: Familiar Territory – Keisha Elle

Footsteps were heard in the distance, becoming closer with each step. Asanti turned to see who was coming up behind her. It was Jace, gaining momentum and on her in seconds.

"We need to talk," Jace said. "Not here."

"Right here is perfect," Rico chimed in. "She already ruined what I had going on."

"She didn't force you to put your dick in another woman, let alone cum inside her. How could you be so stupid? You did that on your own. Stop blaming Asanti for your actions. You're asshole, not her!" Komiko exclaimed.

"I can't believe either one of you." Jace's deep voice silenced everyone. He coldly glowered at Rico. "You're supposed to be my boy."

"You're gonna let a bitch come between our friendship? You're going to just ignore the bro code? What

She's About That Life: Familiar Territory – Keisha Elle

ever happened to bros before hoes. She wanted to make some money and I gave her the stage to do it."

"You're not going to keep calling me out of my name Rico." Asanti scolded. "I know you're mad, but don't direct your anger towards me."

"Fuck you! You're not innocent in all of this!" Rico yelled.

"Don't talk to her like that." Jace said, still feeling like her protector.

"I've heard enough." Komiko fidgeted with her oversized purse. "Asanti, I'll see you at home." She hugged her friend tightly. "Thank you for opening my eyes to what I couldn't see for myself."

"This shit is crazy." Rico threw his hands up in frustration.

She's About That Life: Familiar Territory – Keisha Elle

"You did it to yourself." Komiko shot back.

"Since she wants to run her mouth, why don't you ask her the full story?" Rico asked, ready to expose a secret of his own. If he was going out, he was dragging Asanti right along with him.

"Speak your mind." Jace said, his nostrils flaring.

"Don't listen to him. He doesn't know what he's talking about." Asanti was ready to throw Rico straight under the bus.

"You don't have to listen to me. Ask her yourself. Ask her how it felt to be on her knees with my dick in her mouth."

Asanti knew it was over. She could feel three pairs of eyes burning a hole straight through her. Komiko pleaded with her eyes, begging Asanti to say it wasn't true. She couldn't.

She's About That Life: Familiar Territory – Keisha Elle

"Asanti. Is that true?"

Asanti didn't say a word.

"Asanti! She's talking to you." Jace scolded, hoping for the same denial Komiko was searching for.

There was nowhere to run. She had nowhere to hide. The one thing that she dreaded most in the world was finally coming true. She was front and center. It was time to face the music.

"It's true."

"You, bitch!" Komiko lunged at Asanti's face. She was able to grip a big wad of hair as they both fell to the ground from the impact. "I trusted you."

No more words were spoken. Asanti realized that Komiko was out for blood. Komiko swung wildly, connecting with Asanti's body. Asanti needed to protect herself. Fighting back, she pushed Komiko off of her, gaining the upper hand. Asanti didn't want to hurt Komiko, but if a fight was what she wanted, a fight was what she was going to get. One thing she learned from growing up in the streets of Louisville, KY was how to fight. She was back on her feet ready to go to war. Asanti landed blow after blow in an attempt to stop Komiko's fury.

Komiko backed up in defeat when her swollen eye began to throb. She tasted the salty red blood oozing out of a fresh cut on her lip.

"I want you out of my apartment," she said, stumbling to her feet. "Get all your shit and leave my fucking key. I don't want to see your face ever again."

A struggle broke out behind them. Jace had Rico pinned to the ground. He repeatedly hit Rico with stiff, precise blows. Their brotherhood was forever broken.

She's About That Life: Familiar Territory – Keisha Elle

Determined to leave his mark, Jace continued through Rico's protest.

"Jace, no!" Raven yelled, running down the hall in her Christian Louboutins.

Just like the scavenger she was, Raven was there to pick up the pieces. She grabbed Jace firmly by the arm.

"You're a lawyer! You have an image to uphold. He's not worth it. It's not worth your career."

Jace stopped at Raven's urging. He stood to his feet and brushed himself off. When his eyes met Asanti's, he gave her a hard glare.

"You really had me going. I thought we had something special. Never again. Fool me once, shame on you. Fool me twice, shame on me."

She's About That Life: Familiar Territory – Keisha Elle

He walked away with Raven and Komiko by his side. It was over. Asanti looked at a battered and bruised Rico grimacing in pain. Even in his defenseless state, he still had a mouthful to say.

"Get the fuck out of my spot."

His words took her over the edge. In just a few hours, she had lost her relationship with her best friend and her man. Rico was an easy target. She unleashed the rest of her built up emotions on him. Big Zeke and a few other trusted goons made their way to Rico's side, just as Asanti landed a swift kick to his midsection.

"This is all your fucking fault, you bastard!"

"Calm down Duchess," Big Zeke said, blocking her attempt at another kick. "Do you know what you're doing?"

She's About That Life: Familiar Territory – Keisha Elle

"Escort that bitch out," Rico commanded. "Throw her ass out like the trash she is."

With her chest heaving up and down, she knew it was over. Nothing would ever be the same again. Taking the walk of shame down the long hallway, she gladly exited Club Fantasy before Big Zeke did it for her.

The End

She's About That Life: Familiar Territory – Keisha Elle

She's About That Life: Familiar Territory – Keisha Elle

Epilogue

Asanti sat in her car, wondering where she went wrong. The mistakes that she made over her lifetime began to cloud her mind. For the first time in many years, she wished she had her mother close by. She wanted Julissa to wrap her arms around her tightly and tell her that everything would be okay. Asanti knew that would never happen.

She reached in her glovebox and powered on her cell phone. She hoped for a voicemail or text message from Jace, opening up the line of communication. She smiled to herself when her voicemail icon displayed. She pressed it quickly. The first message was from Jace.

I got a call from Sidney. She said that you needed me. What's going on? I've been calling all morning. I can't go to Florida knowing something might be wrong. I'm coming back home. Call me when you get this message.

She's About That Life: Familiar Territory – Keisha Elle

Her heart sank. If only she had received the message before things blew up in her face. She erased the message and went on to the next one. It was from a private number.

Asanti. Answer the phone. It's me. I need to talk to you.

She quickly erased Justin's message. Before she could put the phone down, it vibrated in her palm. The word PRIVATE appeared on the screen. She slid the green phone icon to the left and answered the call in one swift motion.

"What do you want?"

"Are you okay?" Justin's voice was full of concern.

"Right now is not a good time."

She's About That Life: Familiar Territory – Keisha Elle

"I know, I saw what happened. I just wanted to make sure you were okay."

"How do you know about that?"

"Just because I'm not seen doesn't mean I'm not there. Like now, I see you, sitting in a black BMW with a green bag in your lap."

Asanti looked around, paranoid. Justin was there. She didn't know where, but he was close enough to see what she was doing.

"Stop looking around girl. I'm not going to do anything to you."

"What do you want Justin?" Asanti asked cautiously.

"I just want to talk to you. I want to know where we went wrong."

She's About That Life: Familiar Territory – Keisha Elle

"I doesn't matter. What's done is done." She sat her green tote in the passenger's seat.

"I want to know."

"You can't be faithful. You have too many women in your life. I couldn't settle for that anymore."

"I was young and stupid. It took losing you for me to realize that. I loved you Asanti. I still love you. Through all the bullshit, all the women, all the ups and downs…I still love you baby."

"Justin, don't…"

Asanti heard her passenger's side door handle click. Someone was attempting to open her door. Justin lowered his head to eye level, revealing his face.

"Open the door Asanti," he said, still talking into the phone.

She's About That Life: Familiar Territory – Keisha Elle

"No."

"Please. Asanti, let's talk."

"Justin, I have to go. I have a lot of stuff to do...Starting with going to get my shit."

"Just let me talk to you. I need you Asanti and right now I think you need me more than you're willing to admit. I know I was out of line the other day, and I apologize. Just unlock the doors so we can talk about things."

Asanti thought about the look on Jace's face when he walked away. He was never going to forgive and she knew it. Sidney had won. It was time to face defeat and take steps towards rebuilding. She leaned back in her seat, resting her head in the headrest. She was out of options. In the same predicament she was in when she left Louisville, she had nothing. The fight inside her slowly diminished. Lifting her hand to press the unlock button, she allowed

Justin to enter. He leaned over and kissed her softly on the cheek. Wiping away the tears slowly creeping down her cheeks, he turned her chin, allowing her eyes to meet his.

"Let's go home," he said before planting a soft kiss on her lips.

She's About That Life: Familiar Territory – Keisha Elle

TEXT UCP TO 22828 TO SUBSCRIBE TO OUR

MAILING LIST

If you would like to join our team, submit the first 3-4

chapters of your completed manuscript to

Submissions.Urbanchapterspub@gmail.com

CPSIA information can be obtained
at www.ICGtesting.com
Printed in the USA
LVOW13s1832180518
577693LV00010B/513/P